INSIDE
DOG'S MIND
JACOB'S JOURNAL

* * *

Michelle Lesley Holland

Michelle Lesley Holland 2018
All rights reserved

No part of this publication may be reproduced, stored in a retrieval system, or transmitted in any form or by any means, without the prior permission in writing of Michelle Holland, nor be otherwise circulated in any form of binding or cover other than that in which it is published and without a similar condition including this condition being imposed on the subsequent purchaser.

Cover design by Sam Wall

ISBN-13: 978-1986813907
ISBN-10: 1986813908

THIS BOOK CONTAINS SCENES OF ANIMAL ABUSE AND IS SUITABLE READING FOR ADULTS ONLY

Thank you to my friends and family for their support and my rescue dogs who gave me the inspiration to write this short story.

Thank you to Lisa Tenzin-Dolma, The International School for Canine Psychology and Behaviour for your continued help and support.
(https://theiscp.com)

I am very proud to be an ISCP dog behaviourist.
(https://www.insideadogsmind.co.uk)

Thank you to Sam Wall who designed the book cover.
(http://www.samwall.com)

50% OF ANY PROFIT FROM THE SALE OF THIS BOOK WILL BE DONATED TO DOG RESCUE'S IN NEED OF HELP.

Chapter 1

✲ ✲ ✲

I START TO TREMBLE. In the distance, I can hear a key turning slowly in the front door. My body is automatically going into panic mode. I have nowhere to escape. There are two doors in this kitchen where I live, and both are closed. It is going to happen again, I know it is and there is nothing I can do about it. I anxiously lick my lips and curl up in fear in the far corner of the kitchen praying the man who calls himself my Dad won't take his temper out on me again.

My body is curled tight in the shape of a ball. I need to make myself invisible. I can hear footsteps coming through the hallway. I pant and tremble. I can feel the thudding of his heavy boots vibrating through the old vinyl flooring where I lay. The door to the kitchen is flung open. I try and stay as still as I can, but my body won't stop shaking. I half open one eye and close it as quick as I can. The tall man who is supposed to be my Dad is looking directly at me, his harsh eyes glaring at me in anger. His lips are pursed tight, now his teeth are showing, and he is growling at me angrily. *Why does he hate me so much?*

Today has been no different to any other day since I have lived here. I am left on my own all day with nothing to do and I get bored. I can't tell the time properly, but I am sure I am left alone from very early morning to early evening. I really do try hard to cross my legs for as long as I can, but sometimes I really struggle. When I need to go to the toilet and can't wait any longer, I have no option but to pee on the old vinyl flooring. I hate going to the toilet where I live and sleep but what else can I do?

I wasn't even fed again this morning. Mum and Dad had been arguing, something about being late for work. They argue and shout at each other regularly and I have heard Mum crying on numerous occasions.

Very early this morning I was literally shoved outside to roam around the stinky, dirty garden and it had felt like an eternity. I'd heard them rushing around inside, my ears had twitched from side to side and the aroma of burnt toast drifted towards my nose making my tummy rumble.

Eventually Mum had let me back into the kitchen and had locked the door in a hurry. She'd rushed around in a panic, continuously looking at her watch, slamming the door to the hallway behind her with great force. I'd looked to where my food bowl sits, it was empty. *No breakfast for me again. Mum didn't even say goodbye. A tear is threatening to erupt.*

Earlier this afternoon, my tummy had been rumbling badly. The rumbling had continued to get louder and louder. I desperately needed to find food to try and stop the horrible and agonizing hunger pains I was feeling. I'd investigated every area of the kitchen looking for any hidden scraps. I'd held my head high in the air with my nose working overtime. I'd been positive I could smell food somewhere. My nose had guided me to the back of the rubbish bin. A piece of burnt crust had stared at me invitingly. *Better than nothing.*

Within a split second it was gone. I'd continued to look around and sniffed every inch of the floor. I knew I needed to get onto the top of the work surfaces. I could smell something delicious teasing me from way up high. I'd jumped for all I was worth, but my legs could not manage the height. They're not strong enough, or powerful enough yet and with every jump I failed. On my last attempt, I'd fallen over backwards, landing in my own pee, literally skidding across the vinyl floor, finally coming to a halt against the washing machine with a bang. I could smell urine all over my body and as usual, it made me feel dirty and sick.

Back to the present moment. I open my eyes to see Dad flinging his arms around in the air in anger. He is growling lots of horrible words. I close my eyes tight. I know what is coming next. I curl my body tighter and tighter. I cry out as I feel a blow to my head, my eyes are going from side to side with the force of the impact. I hold my breath. A firm, strong hand is picking me up by the scruff of my neck. I yelp in horror and pain. I keep my eyes tightly closed. My body is going higher and higher. I hear the key turn in the back door, the handle is pulled down, the door is creaking and suddenly I am flying outside.

Here we go again. I brace myself for the impact as my body hits the ground. *Bang.* I yelp again as my body hits the hard ground. I need to stay still. I need to get my breath back. I am too scared to move. My poor head is pounding. *What if he comes back to hit me again?* I gingerly open my eyes. I blink hard as they adjust to the strong sunlight. The evening sun feels warm and healing on my tender body. I cautiously lift my head and sigh with relief to see the back door is closed. I gingerly get up on my four paws. I wobble, I feel unsteady and weak through hunger and pain. I just need to take my time. I put my left front leg forward and thankfully my other three legs join in. I walk a few steps, but my head is still pounding, I feel dizzy and slump down into the grass. *Maybe I need to toughen up?* I am getting used to these daily beatings and abuse. *Is this going to happen to me every day for the rest of my life? Why me? What have I done?*

Chapter 2

* * *

MY SO CALLED MUM isn't much help either. Both her and my Dad have not realised I have feelings too. I am supposed to be part of their family. I want to be loved, walked and played with. I need food and water. *Is this too much to ask for?*

I think I have been here for nearly two months but to be honest I have lost count of the days. Every day is just the same as the one before with me constantly living in fear. The days and nights are so long. It feels as though I have been here forever. I rest my head down and close my eyes. A heavy feeling of tiredness overwhelms me. I am drifting off into a very deep sleep. *I have a flicker of a flashback from my past.*

I can vaguely remember my real Mum. Her gentle tongue would lick me as I suckled on her teats, her warm and tasty milk sliding down my throat. My brothers and sisters close by. *I smile to myself.* How happy I had been back then with my real Mum and my siblings. I'd always felt safe and loved. I had two brothers and two sisters who were all the same colour as me. My mum had a human Mum, and she had a human Mum too who was quite a nice lady. She had three human children and was always running around like a crazy lady trying to do so many different things all at the same time.

The children were all different sizes. One crawled around on the floor, the second one was the same height as me if I were to stand on my hind legs and the third one was nearly the size of my human Nan. I haven't a clue how old they are in human years or how old they would be in dog years, apart from the smaller one who would crawl around the floor, I would say he was a cheeky puppy.

To our relief, we only had to put up with these children once a day. When they did appear, everything got chaotic very quickly. Their favourite game was to pull our ears, grab our tails, and scream loudly as they ran around like lunatics. The cheeky puppy would crawl around at great speed trying to catch us too. Two of them would jump high on the furniture bouncing up and down shouting loudly as they tried to catch us. We always tried our hardest to escape their grasps by jumping off as quickly as we could, but they continued to dive to the left and to the right always trying their hardest to squash us. We quickly learnt to watch their body language. As soon as we could see an attack was imminent, we would move out of their way like a flash of lightning.

Thankfully we could run and swerve a lot faster than they could, although for some reason this made them even more determined to catch us. Eventually their Mum would hear the commotion, rush in, and take them away. We could then relax.

I had so much fun with my brothers and sisters. We were very good at getting up to lots of mischief. We would play fight and run around chasing each other as fast as we possibly could. We'd bite each other on the ears and tails, eventually landing flat on our backs rolling around with one on top of the other. When our play fighting got out of control, our Mum would immediately separate us and tell us off. We knew when Mum really meant it and always obeyed her immediately.

One day whilst we were playing, a strange human walked into the room where we lived. I'd heard my human Nan say, 'They have just turned eight weeks old.' The next moment my Nan had picked up one of my brothers and handed him to this strange person. The person had then walked away with one of my brothers and he never came back. Later that day, the same thing happened again. This time someone took one of my sisters and she never came back. My Mum seemed to be confused and upset. I saw a single tear roll down her face. I'd snuggled up as close as I could to comfort her.

Two days later we heard strange voices again. This time my other brother and sister were taken away and they never came back either. Just me and Mum left now. To say I was confused was an understatement. I had tears rolling down my face. *Where had my brothers and sisters gone?* My mum had looked very sad and my heart was breaking to see her in this state. I'd made sure I stuck to her like glue.

The following morning, I'd heard a strange voice coming from the other side of the door and in walked my human Nan, closely followed by a very tall chunky looking man with a smaller lady just behind him. I'd looked them up and down. The man wore big black dirty boots, scruffy jeans and was wearing a black hoodie. He had a beard and smelt of something odd. The lady was not as tall. She looked scrawny and her hair was not groomed properly. She wore a pair of jeans with lots of holes in them, and a baggy old t-shirt with holes in that too. *How very strange, she must get very cold with all these holes in her clothes.* Her claws were very strange on both of her hands and her feet. I know some people think us dogs are colour blind, but I can tell you now, they were painted in all different colours. The claws on her hands were very long and needed clipping. She had spoken first, 'Yes, ok we'll take him off your hands.' The tall man responded in a deep, harsh voice, 'You just remember what I told you Brenda, you want it, you look after it. I haven't got time to deal with an animal.'

For a split second, I'd seen a very concerned look appear on my Nan's face but at that precise moment, Brenda had pulled some money out from a pocket in her jeans. She'd handed it straight to my Nan. Brenda had then scooped me into her arms and informed me she was going to be by new Mum. I heard my real Mum whimpering as I was carried away. I'd glanced back at her. Tears were rolling down her face. My eyes had filled with tears too and I'd whimpered to her, *'I love you Mum.'*

My new Mum had said we were going home in the boot of their car and within minutes I was sitting in the boot of this metal thing you humans call a car. The sensation was truly scary as it started moving. It was very noisy too. My new Mum and Dad were arguing. Something was making my nose twitch. My nose was high in the air. This swirly stuff was coming towards me. I'd gasped as circles of smoke covered my head. I'd coughed loudly, and my eyes had been stinging. *Whatever were they blowing at me?* At that precise moment I'd felt completely trapped. I was scared and wet myself. Urine dribbled down my leg. I'd tried to look out of the window but all I could see was blue sky and fluffy clouds. After twenty minutes or so the car had come to an abrupt halt.

Mum had opened the boot of the car, looking at me with a big smile on her face, but the smile instantly disappeared when she realised I'd wet myself. The big scary man, my Dad was standing behind her growling angrily. 'You had better clean that bloody mess up straight away, I hope it isn't going to piss and shit everywhere, if it does, I will tell you now, it won't be staying.' I hadn't liked this man from the moment I saw him. *I cannot believe he called me it?* A horrible feeling churned deep down in the pit of my stomach. I longed for my real Mum. I was scared and whimpered quietly to myself.

My new Mum had scooped me up into her arms and at the same time she'd let out a big, long sigh. I'd had the chance to see her face close-up for the very first time. She looked tired and drained, deep wrinkle lines covered her face and her body smelt really disgusting. She most definitely needed a wash. *Maybe she wets herself too?* She carried me into the kitchen, giving me a chance to glance around. The kitchen cupboards were wooden and old looking. Unwashed plates, dishes and cups piled high in the sink. An old table with 3 plastic chairs leant against a half-painted wall to the left, littered with newspapers and junk. The kitchen surfaces looked dirty and cluttered. I didn't have time to see anything else as she placed me down onto the floor and opened another door. I saw green grass outside and my nose had instantly started to twitch. *So many new smells.*

'Come on Jacob,' she'd called. I'd looked around confused. *Who was Jacob?* I'd looked to the left and to the right, but I couldn't see anyone anywhere. *How bizarre.* Mum had stood in the garden facing me. I'd looked at the small two steps leading down to the grass. Without any hesitation I'd jumped both steps in one go from a complete standstill and ran around happily barking until my horrible Dad appeared at the kitchen door shouting, 'Shut that bloody thing up, will you?' Mum had sighed again and for a split second she'd looked very sad. 'Come on Jacob, let's go inside.' I'd looked around but couldn't see anyone else anywhere. *Whoever is this Jacob?*

It really did take me a while to realise Jacob was in fact, my name. I am only a puppy, not even eight weeks old and that is how I came to live here.

Chapter 3

*** * ***

I AM JOLTED BACK to the present moment by a soft kind voice. A face is looking at me from over the garden fence. A lady with a very warm smile and soft blonde hair is whispering, 'Hey little guy, are you ok? Have you been hurt again?' I look up into her beautiful brown eyes and let out a whimper. She is nodding at me as if she understands what I am trying to tell her. 'Don't worry boy, I have got my eye on things. I am going to be looking out for you.'

I walk slowly towards the closed door. I hear the *beep, beep, beep* of the microwave. This noise really hurts my ears. I want to get to it, bite it and shut it up once and for all. My parents use it a lot. Dad puts food in there all the time. He always throws me outside with a slap or two, before he turns on the annoying microwave. He then sits and stuffs his face. He really is greedy and has never even given me a crumb. I feel angry. Maybe I need to start standing up to him. I can smell the aroma of chicken, and my tummy is rumbling again. I feel as if I have a dark cloud hanging permanently over me. I feel lonely and sad. I know I am feeling sorry for myself, but I can't help it.

I wander around the garden to have a sniff around. The garden isn't very big, so it doesn't take me long. I have looked and searched every day since I have lived here to try and find a way to escape. I desperately want to run back home to my real Mum.

'Here lad,' I hear a familiar soft voice whisper, 'Here is some chicken for you.' She is gently throwing pieces of cooked chicken over the fence towards me. I cannot believe it. *Food.* I wolf it down in one go. 'Poor lad, you really are starving, aren't you?' She disappears. I sit patiently waiting for her head to peer over the fence again, but it doesn't. I instantly feel sad and lonely again.

I wander to the shady area of the garden. My mouth is dry. I really am thirsty. Luckily for me we had heavy rain yesterday. I nibble away on the thicker strands of grass, I can taste rain water, but it is not enough to quench my thirst. I desperately need a very long drink of fresh cold water.

I can hear the back door opening and anxiously turn around. Mum is standing there. I sigh with relief. *I thought it might be him again.* 'Jacob come,' she is commanding in an angry voice. I do as she asks and as gingerly as I can, I slowly take the first step and wince as I climb the second step. I realise now how much my body is hurting. She has me by the scruff of my neck. I yelp out in pain. 'Look at this mess,' she is screaming at me. 'You are a naughty, naughty boy. You dirty, dirty dog.' She is pushing my nose into my own poo. I try desperately to wriggle out of her grasp and turn my face away, but she won't stop. She is hurting me. *Enough is enough.* I am desperate and broken and need to get away to safety. I am in so much pain and open my mouth, turn my head and sink my teeth as hard as I possibly can into her ankle, she screams out loudly. At last I am free. I hobble back outside as quickly as my body will allow and curl up in the corner of the garden trying to make myself look invisible again.

I haven't a clue what had come over me. I can hear shouting and banging coming from inside the kitchen. I cringe. Tears are running down my face. I glance up to see my kind lady looking directly at me from over the fence. She has a pitiful look on her face and disappears again. More tears follow and roll down my face.

Mum appears within minutes. She is glaring at me. 'You ever bite me again Jacob, and you will be very, very sorry. You are lucky I haven't told your Dad. If I'd have told him, you would be dead under that grass by now, do you hear me? You can stay out here until you've learned some manners.' My poor body is shaking uncontrollably. I feel terrified. *What does she mean, I would be dead?* She chucks my small metal food bowl onto the floor and throws a handful of those horrible dried biscuits towards it, half of them miss my bowl completely. 'You should count yourself lucky I am giving you any food at all after your behaviour,' she is snarling at me. She turns on her heels and strides back towards the house, the door slamming behind her. Why doesn't she realise these biscuits are horrible and hurt my teeth? I would like to see my so-called parents eat this horrible food every day, maybe then they would understand exactly how I feel.

I drag myself up and walk over to the bowl. My gut instinct is telling me I must eat whether I like it or not as I really don't know when I will get my next meal. I slowly crunch on the biscuits. I feel like I am crunching on stones. They are dry and hard and make me feel so thirsty. I finish off the odd biscuits lying around until I can find no more.

Plop, something has landed next to me. My nose is working overtime. I can smell fresh chicken. I glance over to see my kind lady smiling over the fence. She throws another piece of chicken, it lands right by shoulder. She is holding her finger up to her lip. I am assuming she is asking me not to bark. I wag my tail gratefully, gulping the chicken down which takes all of two seconds. I eagerly look around for her, but she's gone. A big wave of sadness engulfs me.

I am bored again. I walk towards the back door and gently tap my paw on the door. I have been on my own all day. I want to go back inside now. I am startled by a loud bang coming from the kitchen window. Mum is shouting, 'You can bloody stay out there until you have learned your lesson.' With my tail between my legs I wander back to the corner of the garden and plonk myself down with a very big sigh.

I can see Mum looking at me through the kitchen window smoking her cigarette. *Disgusting habit,* I think to myself. I look up again and she has gone. I get up and sniff around the garden. I am pretty sure I can still smell chicken somewhere. I reach the spot where my nose has led me to, but I can't see any chicken anywhere. Maybe it is hiding in the grass. With my two front paws, I gently scratch the grass, I can smell the chicken. It is here somewhere. I sniff and sneeze. I continue to dig and for the first time today I start to feel happy. *I am going to find you Mr Chicken*, I laugh to myself. My legs are achy after my earlier landing, but I carry on. Soil is flying everywhere and for once I am beginning to have fun.

I freeze to the spot. My horrible Dad is standing at the door shouting at the top of his voice. 'Stop it, you little piece of shit.' He is walking directly towards me. *Thud, thud, thud*, I cower and turn my head away. He has me by the scruff of my neck again. I yelp, and wriggle frantically attempting to break free, but I can't. He is just too strong. I keep trying to free myself as he strides towards the kitchen door. I am lifted high into the air and cannot escape. I yelp in pain as he throws me onto the kitchen floor. I slide across the vinyl flooring until I come to a sudden halt with a loud thud against a kitchen cupboard. I wince on impact. I glance up. Mum is standing at the door. She looks different. *Has she been crying too?* One of her eyes is half closed. It looks red and black in colour. 'Stop it you bully,' she is screaming at Dad, 'You can do whatever you want to me but leave Jacob out of it, he's just a baby.'

Dad is glaring at Mum. I can see his face getting redder and redder. 'You both get what you bloody deserve.' His face is too close to hers for my liking and I start to panic. 'I am off to the pub and the two of you had better be out of my bloody way by the time I get home.' He strides away slamming the door behind him with a loud bang.

Mum is sinking onto the floor. She has tears rolling down her face and is sobbing uncontrollably. *This is all my fault,* I think to myself. I must get up. Slowly and gingerly I walk towards her. I nudge her and lick a tear from her face. She lifts her head. I am shocked to see her tearful and painful eye. She is gazing back at me, speaking soft words muffled in between stifled sobs. 'Jacob, I am so sorry, I bought you here. I thought by you being here, he would change, but it has made him worse and you don't deserve any of this. I am so, so sorry.' For the very first time, she opens her arms invitingly, swoops me into her body and holds me tight. I snuggle into her as close I can. Her body feels warm and my body is moving in unison with her cries. At this precise moment, I feel loved again.

Chapter 4

* * *

TWO DAYS HAVE GONE BY and I have kept my head low. Mum has been at home constantly. She still cannot see out of one eye. It looks awful, it is very bruised and swollen. I must admit, I am very happy she hasn't gone to work. I have the full run of the kitchen and garden. I have also been fed and watered regularly. I am feeling much happier in myself and my body feels less achy. When Dad comes home, Mum shuts me out in the garden. She has said it is for my own good and safety. Like me, she seems scared of Dad too. *I hate him.*

My kind lady has been popping her head over the garden fence on a very regular basis. She continues to throw me chicken when the coast is clear.

I have just strolled back into the kitchen from the garden. Mum is coming towards me with this funny looking machine. It looks like a monster to me. Out of the blue, it makes a very loud noise. *Mum is in danger. I need to save her.* I dig my teeth into the edge of this monster. *I need to get it off her.* The noise stops. 'I am trying to hoover Jacob, please don't get in my way. I am really not in the mood.' The noise starts again. *Don't worry Mum, I am on the case.* The noise stops again. Mum has me by the scruff of the neck and is throwing me out into the garden. I land with a bang AGAIN. *I do not understand what I have done wrong?* I just wanted to save her from getting hurt. I wince and lick my wounds.

A whole week has gone by and Dad has kept out of my way. Today though, is different. Mum has told me she is going back to work. I am feeling very sad. I have enjoyed having her company. 7.00am and the house is empty. My parents have left me all alone. I am shut in the kitchen with no breakfast but at least I have a small bowl of water.

The hunger pains have once again returned. I sniff around the kitchen. I can smell crumbs way above me on the kitchen surfaces. I stand back and look. It is just too high for me to reach. I sigh. My eyes focus on a tea towel hanging from the work top. I grab it with my teeth, and shake my head as hard as I can, out of nowhere a teaspoon nearly lands on my head. *No food. Oh well.* I shake the tea towel to the left and to the right. This is great fun. I throw it up into the air and catch it on the way down. I run up and down the kitchen playing catch. I stop and stand as still as a statue, I can feel my fur rising on the back of my neck. I can hear a key in the front door. I can just about recognise my parent's voices. Mum, is saying, 'Ok, but this really is your last chance. You need to start making more of an effort. I mean it, or I will be out of here for good.' I hear him grunt, 'Ok.'

Mum opens the door and is looking around. 'Good boy Jacob, you haven't been to the toilet in here today, well done.' Suddenly, I feel like a king. 'You have pinched my tea-towel though?' I freeze again but she smiles. 'We are going to take you out for a ride in the car.'

I am not too sure about this. I watch as she picks up a long piece of thin leather. I cower as she comes towards me. She totally ignores my body language. *Can she not see how scared I am?* 'Come on Jacob, let's go.' She is clipping this leather strap thing onto my collar. She starts to drag me. *Why is she doing this?* My neck and throat are hurting. I am still bruised from the recent events and feel as if I am choking. I shake my head as hard as I can as I try to get this thing off me, but she just continues to pull me through the hallway. I yelp out in pain.

I can see the front door is open. I put my head out and point my nose high into the air. I can smell hundreds of different scents all at once. Grumpy Dad spoils things once again. 'Come on, hurry up and get it in the car,' he is shouting. Mum is pulling me again. I jump up and bite the leather strap and pull it as hard as I can. Mum is trying her best to free my teeth off the strap and is struggling to get me under control. The tone of his voice stops me in my tracks, 'Bloody hurry up woman.' *Thud, thud, thud*, I shake. *I hate the sound of those boots.* I cower instantly waiting for his next move. He has me by the scruff of my neck and is literally throwing me into the boot of the car. I look around for my Mum. I can see she is in the front left side of the car. I am relieved and wag my tail in happiness knowing she is safe.

At this precise moment I feel the most excruciating pain I have ever felt in the whole of my short life. I yelp out loudly. I cry in agony. I can't explain how awful this pain feels. It is shooting through the whole of my body. I can't move. I am stuck. Mum is hysterical. 'What the bloody hell have you done to Jacob?' Dad is opening the boot. I can see a look of shock across his face. Mum looks white and anxious. I watch in disbelief as half of my tail drops to the ground. 'You, stupid, horrible man, look what you have done.' Dad is still not moving. I have never seen him so quiet. 'Quick, get it inside before the neighbour's report us,' he is gasping.

Immediately Mum scoops me into her arms. I yelp again in pain, I am trembling with shock. I can hear a familiar gentle voice and slowly lift my head to see my kind lady rushing towards the car. 'Is your dog ok? What has happened? Please let me see him.'

Mum is holding me tight, rushing to get me inside as quickly as she can. I can hear Dad shouting 'Get back into your house and mind your own bloody business. You are a nosey old cow. I trod on his foot that's all.'

I am in excruciating pain. *My tail, where is the other half of my tail?*

Mum has not put me down. I can feel her heart racing very, very fast. She is holding me tight and crying. 'What are we going to do?' she cries as Dad appears. 'We need to get him to a vet.' 'We are not taking it to the bloody vets. We can't afford it, just bandage it up woman. It is only a bit of tail. I will get rid of the other piece. Now get a grip and do as I bloody tell you.' The door bangs and he is gone.

Mum is sobbing loudly. She is holding me under one arm and rummaging through the cupboards with the other hand. Eventually she pulls out a crepe bandage. She gently places me on the kitchen floor and tenderly wraps the bandage around what is left of my tail as tightly as she can. I yelp and cry out. The pain is piercing and agonizing.

I am trembling and shaking, my body is in complete shock. At last she has finished dressing with my tail and slumps slowly to the floor. *She must be in shock too*. She is gently picking me up and holding me close. I can see my blood splattered over her clothes and on her hands. She is stroking my head and kissing me. At this precise moment I feel safe. I don't ever want her to let me go.

We have been sitting here seemingly for a very long time. There is no light on in the kitchen and it is getting dark. I really need some pain relief. Mum gently gets up and carries me out to the garden. She carefully puts me on the grass and I instantly pee. She is standing over me, watching me closely. She has never done this before. For a split second, I am sure I see my kind lady at the fence. *I must be hallucinating.* Mum picks me up and carries me back into the kitchen, gently placing me on the floor. I watch as she opens a cupboard. I can hear a tin being opened. I watch closely as she picks up my food bowl. My nose is high in the air. 'Here you are Jacob. A special treat just for you. I hope it makes you feel a little bit better,' she is saying in a very soft voice. The bowl is right in front of me. *Tuna. Wow.* I tuck in and it is gone in a flash. I wag my tail but the intense pain I feel stops me immediately. 'Oh, Jacob, please try your hardest not to wag. You have made it bleed again.' She reaches for another bandage and wraps it on top of the existing one. I yelp again in pain. I feel sick.

She disappears for a few minutes and I wait anxiously for her to return. *Here she is*, walking towards me carrying some towels and for the first time ever, she makes a cosy bed for me in the corner of the kitchen. I am used to laying on the cold floor. I snuggle down. She strokes my head. An overwhelming feeling of tiredness is sweeping over me and I cannot keep my eyes open any longer. I dream of running across beautiful green fields chasing a ball and playing with my brother and sisters. My eyes shoot open and I am back to reality. My tail is throbbing. I instantly remember everything that happened earlier and whimper.

Chapter 5

* * *

TWO WEEKS HAVE GONE BY since that awful incident with my tail and Mum has been so much nicer to me. She's even given me fresh chicken a few times. Dad has tried to keep out of my way. He detests me. I don't know why as I have never done anything bad to him. When he walks into the kitchen, I cower. He smirks. When he moves a hand, I cower. He smirks. *I really do hate him. Is that a horrible thing to say?* What is left of my tail is healing slowly. It is a good job border collie's like me are tough. My kind lady from next door has also been keeping an eye on me. When my human parents aren't around she smiles and throws me chicken. *I wish with all of my heart I could go and I live with her.*

Today, Mum has left earlier than usual. She did let me out to go to the toilet before she went and even left some biscuits in my bowl. I hear the door slam. I sigh with relief. Horrible Dad has gone to work too. At least for now I can relax. I start to crunch on my biscuits. 'Yuk.' I paw at the bowl and some of the biscuits roll across the kitchen floor. I use my paws to roll them around. I skid around on the vinyl floor, this is great fun. Out of the corner of my left eye, I can see something moving. I prowl slowly across the kitchen like a panther. I stop. I can see something very small wriggling and slithering around. I bark at the imposter. He takes no notice. On closer inspection, I see it is a maggot. *Yikes.* I need to keep an eye on where he is going. I bark at him again. I play bow, but he is totally ignoring me. I bound towards him again. He is making his way to the corner of the kitchen and is getting far too close to my bed for my liking. *Oh no you don't.* I pounce on him. I miss and now I can't see him. *I hope he isn't in my bed?* I dig at my towels. *Where has he gone*? I start to dig the corner of the vinyl floor looking for it, a bit like I do in the garden. *He must be hiding under here somewhere?* I can see a loose piece of vinyl. I grab it and pull as hard as I can, clenching my teeth tight. I am determined to find him. I pull hard at another large piece of vinyl to reveal an old wooden floor with crumbs scattered around. I lick them up as fast as I can and start to dig again. *I am now on a mission.*

It doesn't take me long to realise half of the floor is now old wood. I still can't find the maggot. I rip and shred the vinyl as fast as I can, licking up any crumbs I find on my way. Suddenly, I am positive I can smell chicken. I start to search. *Found it!* To my complete horror, it is covered in green mould and is moving. The naughty maggot and his friends are wriggling around on the chicken. For a second, I feel sick. I need the toilet. I cock my leg and pee over the maggots and laugh to myself. *Take that you bunch of imposters.* None of them move. I smile. *Oh no, they are moving again.* I bark and jump as close as I can to them, but they are not taking any notice of me. I am concentrating on them so much, I don't hear the door open. I am caught totally off guard.

Dad is standing with his hands on his hips looking at the chaos in the kitchen. *I was only trying to help by getting rid of the imposters. Surely, he can see that*? He is glaring at me. I walk backwards. 'You are a naughty little shit. What the bloody hell have you done to my kitchen?' His fists are clenched tightly, and he looks as if he is about to explode. I am shaking as the *thud, thud, thud* of his boots, come towards me. I curl myself up in the corner on the wooden floor and brace myself. *'Ouch,'* a boot has got me in my ribs. *'Ouch,'* a blow to my head. His hand is grabbing my neck. I twist and turn my body trying to escape from his strong grasp. I wriggle and turn around to bite him in self-defence. *Wrong move.* 'Don't you ever try to bite me ever again. You are a horrible piece of crap. You deserve to be punished.'

I remember my Mum's words the day I had bitten her. *Is he going to kill me?* My neck is really hurting. I feel a sensation of being lifted high above the ground. I keep my eyes tightly closed. I can hear the door open and I am soaring through the air. It seems like an eternity. I land with a thump against the fence. I yelp out in pain. I am winded and cannot move. I try to breathe slowly but my chest feels tight and pains are shooting through it. I keep my eyes closed. I am too scared to open them. 'You little shit, you can stay out there until you learn some manners.' I can hear the kitchen door slam shut. I still daren't open my eyes. I need to lay here for a while. 'OMG, look at you my poor darling.' I hear the gentle voice of my kind lady. I slowly open my eyes to see her face peering over the fence at me. I let out a whimper. 'This is never, ever going to happen to you ever again. I promise you. Trust me.' I try to lift my head to see where she has gone but even this is an effort. *Where is my Mum?* I could really do with a cuddle. My body is throbbing in agony and my head is pounding. I should be used to the regular abuse by now. I loathe the pain I am forced to endure.

I have now been lying here for what seems hours. My body feels as though it has broken into a thousand tiny pieces.

I can vaguely hear the back door open. I wince as I lift my head. I am shocked to see a strange lady looking directly at me. She is wearing a black uniform and holding a clip board. I watch as she puts the clip board onto the step. She is walking towards me. I curl my lip and growl. My body cannot cope with any more beatings today. 'Hey, I am not going to hurt you,' she is talking in a very soft voice. I cower and shake again. 'I will be back in a moment.' I watch as she walks towards the kitchen picking up her clip board on her way and closes the door behind her. I can hear her talking to Dad. A short while later, I hear the door open. The lady in black is looking at me in a very sad way. My kind lady is looking over the fence. She whispers, 'You will be safe now, I promise. This nice lady is going to take you away from that nasty man and look after you.' I am confused. *What does she mean?*

I can hear Dad shouting out to the lady in black, 'Take the little shit, good riddance I say. Hurry up and piss off out of here.' 'Mr Pollard, there is no need to shout and use language like that. You have signed your dog over into my care. Now please leave us alone,' she is speaking in a very calm manner and for once Dad doesn't answer back.

'Jacob, you poor, poor love. I am not going to hurt you, I promise,' she is saying in a gentle voice. 'I am going to take you somewhere safe. Please trust me.' My kind lady next door had told me to trust her, *but can I?* I am not sure I can trust anyone anymore. She is taking a step closer. I growl and shake. 'Come on boy, we need to get you out of here.' I really haven't a clue what is going on. She moves her hand. I close my eyes waiting for the strike, but it doesn't come.

I can smell some food close by. I open my eyes. She is throwing me treats. One has landed right by my front paw. I move my achy head. I need to keep one eye on this lady who is suddenly sitting on the grass. She is probably sitting in my poo, but she doesn't seem to be bothered. *Poor lady.* I have never had treats that taste this good before. Whatever they are, I love them. Very slowly I try to get up. I need to get to the rest of these tasty treats. My body is stiff, and my legs are wobbly. The lady in black is talking to me in a very gentle voice. She has laid a trail of tasty treats leading directly to her. 'Come on Jacob. You really are a handsome boy. I promise I am not going to hurt you. I need to get a lead on you, so I can get you out of here.' Her energy is very calm, and I feel myself slowly relaxing. *Is she going to get me out of here? Can she be trusted?*

I slowly eat the treats one by one. I am now getting very close to her. She is holding out her hand and I can smell fresh chicken. I am so hungry. I lean forward. I can nearly reach it but my neck hurts. I need to be brave and take one step closer. I snatch the chicken off her hand and quickly retreat backwards. The lady in black doesn't move. She is opening her other hand to reveal more chicken. 'Good boy Jacob, come on just one more step and I can get a lead on you.' She has thrown the chicken on the grass right next to where she is sitting. My tummy is rumbling with hunger. I slowly move forward and before I know it I have this rope thing around my neck. I panic and yelp as I pull backwards. My body is in so much pain. I haven't got the energy to fight anymore. The lady in black hasn't moved. She is talking to me in a gentle voice, telling me how brave I am. I have finally got my breath back. She has some more chicken in her hand. I gently take it. She is slowly moving backwards, and the rope is straining my neck. She is offering me more chicken. I move forward. *I get it now*. If I follow her and the chicken, the rope doesn't hurt my neck. She isn't rushing me, and slowly, after a few more steps we are inside the kitchen. I stand and look around. It is a complete mess. *Where is Dad?*

I start to shake again. I am terrified he is going to appear and beat me again. The lady distracts me with more chicken and very slowly we make our way through the kitchen. We are in the hallway and I can see the front door is open. *Nearly there*. She is at the front door offering me more chicken. I can't move. I am literally frozen to the spot.

Before I know it, she has scooped me up into her arms and is holding me tight. 'Ouch,' I whimper. My body is hurting so badly. 'We are nearly there Jacob. You really are such a brave boy.' She is opening a big door at the back of a van. I immediately panic. I don't want to lose the rest of my tail. I continue to shake in fear. She opens a cage door and before I know it I am inside on a soft warm bed and she is gently closing the door. I am really confused. *What is happening to me?* I panic and suddenly feel urine running down the inside of my back legs. 'Hey Jacob, please don't be scared. I will have you in a safe place within thirty minutes. I promise.' She slowly closes the door to the van. This van smells of dogs. I can hear the engine start and we are moving. I lay down in my pee. I am completely exhausted and to be honest at this precise moment, I wish I was dead.

I must have drifted off. The van has suddenly stopped, and I am awake and confused. I listen carefully. I can hear maybe three or four different voices outside. In the distance I can hear dogs barking. *What is going to happen to me now?*

Chapter 6

* * *

I CAN HEAR THE DOOR HANDLE TURNING. The door is open. I can see two ladies, a man and the lady who took me, all looking directly at me. I start to tremble. She is opening my cage door and is talking to me in a very gentle voice. The others have moved out of the way. I close my eyes. I really don't care anymore. I am tired, hungry and thirsty. My body feels as though it is completely broken and needs gluing back together. My rescue lady scoops me into her arms and I whimper in pain as she carries me towards a building. I can hear dogs barking and the nearer we get the louder they bark. I am trembling uncontrollably, and I cannot stop. 'Don't worry boy, you will soon be in a lovely warm kennel with a nice warm bed with blankets and delicious food.'

The others are following closely behind, I look back warily. She opens a door to a very large building. We are inside. I can see many kennels and dogs peering at me. So many smells, so many sounds, my senses are again in overdrive. I am on high alert. We climb some steps and eventually reach the end of the kennel block. She opens another door. I look around. I can see a soft bed with blankets. I can see toys. My eyes are glued to two bowls on the floor. I can immediately see one is full of water and the other looks to contain food. Even though I am tired my nose picks up the most beautiful aroma, *chicken.*

    She gently places me on the floor once she has closed the door behind us. I still can't stop shaking and I feel as though I've lost all control of my body parts. She is sitting on the comfy looking bed, holding out her hand. I can see tasty chicken. I slowly walk towards her. My legs are shaking and wobbling. I am having trouble controlling them. One step, two steps, chicken. I am totally exhausted. She scoops me into her arms. 'Come on boy, I will stay with you until you stop shaking. Look, you have a heater above your bed.' She is wrapping us both up in a warm blanket. This feels good. I can feel the warmth of her body and can hear her heart beating. She is gently stroking my head. 'You are safe now boy, no-one is ever going to hurt you again. I promise.' These words are music to my ears. My eyes are heavy, and I drift off into my first deep sleep in a very long time.

I must have been totally shattered. I don't even remember my rescue lady leaving. I hope she will come back soon. I open my eyes and peer around. My new house is a good size, and thankfully very warm and cosy. I can see the front of my house is made of a kind of plastic material. I can't see anything through it except right at the top there is an area I can peer through. I think I can see a roof. I can hear muffled barks. *Maybe my new house has double glazing?* I can see an archway in the wall at the back of my new home. I hadn't noticed this before. I slowly get up. My legs are weak. My body feels tender and bruised all over. I walk towards the bowl of food and slowly start to eat. *Very tasty. Chicken and vegetables.*

Within minutes I have eaten the lot. I lick the bowl just to check I haven't missed anything. Fresh water. My tongue is lapping up the water so fast it is splashing my face and over my ears, but I don't care. I walk slowly towards the archway. I can see a small concrete area. At the back is a brick wall and there are rectangular windows at the top letting in glimpses of sunlight. I can see a big white door. I walk back to my bed. My little stroll and eating my food has completely worn me out. I haven't a clue what day or time it is. What I do know is, my poor body needs time to recover.

The heat is warm on my back. I snuggle down in my bed and close my eyes. I am woken, totally startled by the door opening and immediately begin to shake. Through habit, I curl myself up into a ball. A small lady is slowly walking in. I can't help it, I wet myself again. I close my eyes and wait for the blow to my body. It doesn't happen. I can hear a soft voice. 'Good boy, I am pleased to see you have eaten all of your breakfast. You had us all worried for a while. You were totally exhausted and have slept for more than eighteen hours.' I open one eye. She has brown hair and is wearing trainers, a pair of jeans and a T-shirt with a picture of a collie on the front. I watch closely as she fills up my food bowl. She is putting something into my food with a syringe. 'This pain relief will really help you. I hear you have had a pretty rough time. You are safe now, so you need to try and relax.' This is what the kind lady over the fence and my rescue lady had both said, *but how do I know I can trust them?* I am so unsure.

'I will be back shortly with some clean bedding and fresh water for you. Try to eat all your dinner as this will help the pain relief to kick in quicker. See you soon.' The door closes. I manage to drag myself out of bed again. My tummy and legs feel wet. I hobble towards my food bowl. My body feels stiff and I eat my food slowly. It truly is delicious. Chicken and flavoured gravy. *How wonderful is this?* What a difference to the hard stone like biscuits I used to have to eat. I lick the bowl clean. *I freeze to the spot.* The door is opening. The same person is walking in. I stand in fear. I cannot stop the urine running down my legs, I've done it again, I've wet myself, I am so anxious. 'Hey Jacob.' *How does she know my name?* 'Please don't feel scared of me, I am here to care for you and to look after you. I am going to put some fresh blankets in your bed and take the wet ones away. Don't worry accidents often happen, and I promise you will feel so much better with a nice clean bed.' *Why isn't she telling me off?* She is walking towards me and I cower. 'I am just going to fill up your water bowl and take your food bowl away.' Her movements are slow, and she is avoiding any eye contact with me. I stay where I am until she has finished. 'I will see you later with your supper and medication. Please try and rest Jacob, you're safe now.' The door closes, and she disappears. I make my way slowly back to my bed. The blankets are warm and smell fresh and comforting. I snuggle down. The heat is on my back, and I can't stop my eyes from closing.

I am awoken once again by the door opening. It is the same lady. I stay still and start to shake immediately. 'Hey Jacob. I bet that sleep did you the world of good. We need to build up your strength.' I watch her closely. She is putting my food bowl onto the floor and has that syringe again. 'Make sure you eat your supper and try and get some sleep. I will see you in the morning.' She slowly walks towards the door and vanishes. I can smell my supper and get up slowly. My body feels a little less painful and I demolish my food in minutes. Delicious, vegetables, chicken and gravy. *Yum, yum. Oh no, now I need a poo.* I haven't had one since I have been here. I walk towards the archway and poo. It is runny and smells disgusting. At least it isn't near my clean bed. I walk back and snuggle down. The warmth on my back feels warm and healing. The lights in my house have gone dark. My eyes are heavy, and I can't stop them from closing. Within seconds I drift off to sleep.

Chapter 7

*** * ***

A FEW DAYS HAVE GONE BY. I am now receiving four regular meals a day and thankfully my aches and pains are tenderly being nursed away. I haven't been out of my new house yet. To be honest, I am quite happy to stay where I am. The same lady has been attending to my daily needs. It is strange as even though I have wet my bed a few times, she hasn't shouted at me once. She just goes off, brings back fresh bedding and smiles at me. *I need to stop wetting myself.*

The door is opening and here she is again. I stay where I am. She is chatting to me in a merry voice. 'Do you know you have been here for nearly two weeks Jacob?' I am shocked to hear this. I thought I had been here for just a few days. 'You are looking much stronger and you have put on a good amount of weight. This is what we were hoping for. How would you feel about going out for some fresh air a bit later?' *To be honest, I am not too sure about this. I would rather stay where I am.* I watch as she does her usual routine and the split second she disappears I head straight to my food bowl. I must say I do love the food I am served.

Here she is again and this time she is holding something in her hands. I watch her cautiously. 'This is a harness Jacob. I am going to put it on you slowly and then we can go outside for a little walk. A nice stroll will do you the world of good.' I cower backwards as she comes towards me. I remember when my Mum said she was taking me for a walk. She'd dragged me by a strap on my neck. I'd felt like I was choking, and my neck and throat had hurt badly. This lady is offering me a treat. I snatch it out of her hand and immediately regret my actions. She doesn't move. When I feel worried or concerned I can't help my bad behaviour and forget my good manners. I just lose all control and I can't help it.

She is leaning forward and putting something over my head. I freeze and start to shake. 'Jacob, you know I am not going to hurt you, I just want to take you for a walk. Please trust me.' She is offering me another treat. I try not to snatch too hard. There you go, good boy. Now I am just going to put two straps under your chest, do them up and we will be ready to go.' To be honest she was so quick I didn't have time realise what she was doing.

She has a long strap thing in her hand. I close my eyes. I anticipate the pain this is going to cause to my neck. I feel nothing. 'Come on boy, off we go.' She is moving, and I am moving but I wonder why can't feel anything on my neck? She opens the back door of my house. I have never been ventured through this door. *I freeze.* My claws are glued to the concrete floor. She gently throws a treat down and I take one step forward. Another treat, another step. She doesn't rush me and soon we are at another door. *I freeze again.* She opens the door and immediately my nose is high in the air. *I can smell so many scents but is it safe for me to go out there?* We play, drop the treat, I eat. I quite like this game as it is taking my mind off everything else around me.

Soon the texture underneath me feels different. I am standing on lush green grass. Smells are all around me and my natural instincts take over. I need to investigate. I think I take her by surprise as I turn and run to the right.

She is running closely behind me and soon I feel a strain on the top of my back and within seconds, she is back at my side.

I look up to see two large dogs coming directly towards us with two strange people. I lunge forward and bark as loud as I can. My handler is trying to get my attention. I ignore her. I need to check out these two dogs. The dog on the left lunges at me and nearly grabs me by the scruff of my neck. I panic and quickly rush back with my half a tail trying to fit under my back legs. I am a little shaken up.

My legs are feeling very weak. My handler is now sitting on the grass and is gently inviting me towards her. She leans forward, and I allow her to gently stroke my chest, as she talks to me in a very soft voice. I get the odd treat too. Once I have managed to stop shaking she gets up. 'Come on Jacob, five more minutes and I will take you back inside. You have done very well for your first time out'. I sniff the grass close by and pee. She seems to be elated. She is patting me, telling me what a good boy I am doing a toilet and gives me another treat. *I have never seen anyone get so excited about me having a pee?* I feel quite proud of myself and lick her hand. 'Aw thank you Jacob, that is so sweet of you.' I look up and she is smiling.

Out of nowhere I suddenly hear a very loud bang. I panic, I need to get to safety. I jolt her arm, but she still has hold of me. I am panting anxiously, and she is trying to keep me calm. My head is high in the air, my nose is working overtime. I need to get back to the safety of my home. In a blind panic I head off in the direction my nose has told my brain I must go. She is struggling to get me under control. *Phew, we are back at the door to my house.*

'Oh Jacob, poor boy. That really did scare you didn't it? It was just a car back firing.' *It is times like this I wish I could speak the human language.*

We are back in my house, she unclips four straps and this harness thing falls to the ground underneath me. I feel mentally worn out and head straight to my water bowl. It is lovely to have clean fresh water and after splashing water everywhere with my thirsty tongue I instantly feel calmer.

She has disappeared. *Where did she go?* I look around and as if by magic she is now standing right in front of me with my dinner. I attempt to wag my half a tail, but to be honest it sometimes still feels tender and I stop immediately. I enjoy my dinner and snuggle down in my nice, warm bed and close my eyes, sighing happily.

Chapter 8

✷ ✷ ✷

ANOTHER WEEK HAS GONE BY and I am still living in my new house. I am receiving regular food and feeling stronger every day. Different people have been popping in to feed me as apparently my regular carer has gone on holiday. There was one specific person who had popped in and he had really scared me. He was tall and had a beard and he reminded me of Dad. I'd growled at him fiercely. He had slid my food bowl along the floor, turned and disappeared in a flash, thankfully I didn't see him again.

This week I've had different humans walking me. I have had to wear my harness twenty- four hours a day, apparently it is until my regular carer gets back. I suppose it makes it easier for the new human walkers and feeders instead of than them having to try and catch me. I don't mind too much as it is quite comfortable. Two days ago, a very smallish human visited my house. She had grey hair and lots of deep wrinkles in her face. She told me she was going to take me for a walk. I had behaved very well until we got outside and what happened next was not really my fault.

Out of the blue I'd seen a cat slowly prowling from out of the bushes. Off I went at 100mph, the poor wrinkly lady was nowhere to be seen although I did hear a yelp behind me. I needed to get the cat, but I couldn't find it. I heard people calling my name, but I ignored them. Sniffing inside the bushes was much more fun.

I even found what was left of an old burger. *I soon demolished that!* Eventually it had started to get dark and I could see some torch lights shining through the bushes. 'Jacob, come on lad, we have your dinner waiting,' several different voices had called. To be honest, I was quite hungry and ready for my dinner, so eventually I decided to make my way back through the bushes towards the lights.

A lady who I had met twice before was waiting for me. She'd leant forward and managed to grab the lead which miraculously was still on the top of my harness. She didn't shout at me at all. She calmly took me back to my nice warm bed and my dinner was served. I'd wondered where the wrinkly lady had gone. *Very strange. I hope she was ok?*

I had a very bad tummy that night, constant diarrhoea. I will never ever eat an old burger again. Lesson learned.

At last, my regular carer is back. I am thrilled to see her, but she looks different. Her skin colour looks darker and her teeth look whiter, I sniff her to be sure. *How bizarre.* 'Jacob, I have a special person who is coming to see you later so please try and be on your best behaviour.' *I wonder who this could be? Maybe it could be my kind lady who used to throw chicken to me over the fence or maybe it could be my Mum?* I do worry about her. I hope she is ok. I really wish she would come and visit me soon.

We walk out onto the field and I suddenly hear a very familiar voice calling my name. I turn my head and I am thrilled to see it is the lady in black who rescued me from my horrible Dad. I cannot contain my excitement. I literally drag my carer behind me at the speed of lightening. I cannot stop and bump right into my rescuer with a bang. Her face is a treat. 'Look at you boy, wow you look so handsome, you have put on so much weight and have so much energy.' She seems elated. I cannot tell you how excited I was to see her. I have so much to thank her for as she took me away from the constant beatings.

My body is moving in all directions. She is laughing. 'Jelly bum is what I am going to call you from now. I am so proud of you boy.' I lick her face and glance up into her eyes. She blinks and smiles. I am sure she knows I am saying a very big thank you.

I sit and look around my house. I have five toys left to play with. My favourite one is a pink pig who grunts when I touch him. *I truly love him.* I gently throw him up into the air and as he lands on the floor, he oinks. He makes me smile. I have had lots of other toys but sadly I've demolished the ones I don't like. One poor giraffe annoyed me so much with his constant squeaking every time I touched him, I really had no option but to rip his head off, find the squeak inside him and destroy. I loved a big soft bear one person had given to me. He was warm and cuddly, and I loved to rest my head on his lovely big belly.

One night I had pulled him into my bed as he always liked to sleep with me. I'd woken up horrified to see I had accidently peed all over him. I had tried my best to clean him up, licking him constantly in the hope that he would be ok. I had then noticed he had a hole in his right leg. I tried to make his leg better by pulling out this white fluffy stuff which was hanging out but then another hole appeared in his tummy. I tried to help again. A hole appeared in his head. I continued to remove all the white fluffy stuff. He was shrinking and shrinking and eventually there was hardly anything left of him. *I really did not mean to kill him.* He turned into a very skinny bear and my house was covered in fluffy white stuff.

Chapter 9

* * *

'JACOB, YOU HAVE NOW BEEN HERE for over three months and you are now fit and well. It is time to find you, your forever home.' I look up into my carer's eyes. *I don't want a new home. I want to stay here.* She carries on talking. 'Last week we published your photo onto our website and have already had five different people enquire about you.' *I really don't like the sound of this and bark directly at her.* She takes no notice. 'We have a lovely couple who are going to take you for a walk later today to see how you all get on. Please try to be on your best behaviour. I will come and fetch you soon.' She disappears. To be honest I am feeling very worried. *What if I get a nasty human to live with again?* I never want to go through that again.

My harness is on and off we go. Two strange humans are walking towards us. I immediately feel uncomfortable and start to tremble. I hear my carer talking. 'Mr & Mrs Cooper?' 'Yes, are you Jane?' I look around. *Who is Jane?* I can't see anyone else nearby. 'She is holding out her hand and the strange human man is moving his hands towards her.' I growl and bark, lunging directly towards him. *There is no way I am going to let my carer get hurt.* My carer acts quickly and moves me away in a flash. The strange man has a surprised look across his face. He is looking at the human woman standing next to him. They both shake their heads at the same time. 'To be honest Jane, he is not going to be the right dog for us. I am so sorry.' *I have just realised my carer's name is Jane.* I look up at her and she looks sad. 'I totally understand your decision, as you know Jacob has been through a really rough time and it is essential we find him his perfect forever home.'

The two humans turn and walk away. *I didn't like him anyway.* Jane lets out a sigh. 'Oh Jacob, what am I going to do with you?' *Take me home with you* is what I want to say. We have our walk and return to my house.

The next day Jane explains another human will be coming to meet me. Every time I see Jane, my body erupts with excitement and my half tail wiggles to the left and to the right at full speed. This always makes her smile. She sometimes calls me Jelly bum like my rescue lady does.

I can see a very tall lady wearing wellingtons, trousers, long coat and a funny looking hat. This time Jane starts to walk the other way, 'Mrs Saunders, hi I'm Jane and this is Jacob, would you like to join us?' The new lady catches up with us and is walking on the other side of Jane. *I most definitely need to keep an eye on this new imposter.* They continue to chat away whilst I enjoy sniffing my lovely surroundings. Out of the blue, we all come to a sudden stop. Jane is sitting on our favourite bench and the new imposter is sitting right next to her. I watch. The imposter is getting something out of her pocket. I can hear the rattle of a packet. My nose is high in the air. She is holding out a treat to me. I hesitate, move quickly forward, snatch the treat out of her hand and move back. She is offering me another one. I snatch it as quick as I can. 'Gently Jacob, where are your manners?' Jane is saying to me. They both get up at the same time and we start walking again.

Something feels different. I look to my left and find that the imposter is now holding my lead. *Oh no, you don't. I need to get away.* I start to run as fast as I can. The imposter is taken completely by surprise and is suddenly running behind me as fast as she can, trying very hard to keep up. I can hear Jane shouting, 'Jacob stop.'

Out of the corner of my eye I can see a seagull sitting on the grass. He is staring directly at me. I divert quickly, and head at full speed towards him. I am running flat out but can't feel any pressure on my lead. *Wow, this imposter must be a very fast runner! I think to myself.* I need to concentrate on the job in hand. I am about two feet away from the seagull when he suddenly takes off and flies off high into the sky.

I can hear Jane calling my name. I stop suddenly and look around. The imposter is nowhere to be seen. I can see Jane far away in the distance and as quickly as I can I turn around and run directly towards her. As I get closer I can see the imposter sitting on the floor. *What is she doing there?* 'Jacob, you pulled Mrs Saunders over and she is shaken up and unfortunately she has hurt her arm.' For a slight second, I feel bad, but it doesn't last for long. I know it is unkind, but I don't want to go and live with her anyway, silly lady. Even dogs know you shouldn't try and run in wellies! Jane has that sad look on her face again and sighs. 'Oh, Jelly Bum. What am I going to do with you?' *Take me home with you,* I scream in my head.

The following day Jane is asking me yet again to be on my very best behaviour. I secretly smirk to myself. I can see two strange people ahead. As we get closer to them Jane nods, turns around and they start to follow us. I glance around. I need to know exactly where they are. The man is close behind us and he is now laughing very loudly to the lady. She starts to laugh too. I suddenly see red and feel very angry. I am positive they are laughing at my half a tail. We carry on walking and immediately I know the man is holding my lead. *Very sneaky, how very dare he?* I turn around as quick as I can, jump up and bite the lead, hanging onto it for dear life. I need to get away from him. Jane has quickly grabbed my lead and is now walking me the other way. Once again, she lets out a huge sigh. Before long we are back in my house. 'Oh dear, Jelly bum. You are not really helping yourself, are you?'

You have turned away everyone we have met. 'Such a shame,' she sighs. For a moment I do feel bad as I know deep in my heart she is only trying to help me. She has already told me I can't live with her as she has three cats and two young children. Maybe I do need to try and behave myself. After all, my own dream of living with Jane can no longer be a reality. I need to find a human of my own.

Chapter 10

* * *

TWO DAYS LATER AND JANE APPEARS AGAIN. I am very excited to see her. 'Today, Jelly bum a lovely lady is coming to walk with us. Any chance you could try and behave?' I look up at her and wiggle my bum. She smiles.

Off we go again. The new lady is standing patiently waiting for us. She is tall and slim and has her hair in a pony-tail. She walks towards us, turns and walks at Jane's side. She has a very soft voice and Jane seems to like her. We walk towards the field and eventually stop. Jane and the new lady sit down together on our favourite bench. The new lady is getting something out of her pocket. I watch carefully. She is opening a metal tin. I can smell chicken. She is offering me a piece. 'Gently Jelly bum,' Jane is saying. I take a step forward and lean my neck as far as I can, but I can't reach. The new lady has dropped the chicken onto the grass only a few inches from me. This has taken me by surprise. I gobble it up in a flash. I look at her to see she is holding another piece of chicken. She drops it onto the grass again and I take a step closer and gobble it up. She is now holding a piece of chicken in the palm of her hand. I am not far away and lean over and take it from her hand and instantly jump backwards. I can hear her saying in a very gentle voice, 'Good boy Jacob, looks like you love chicken?' *How does she know this? She has only just met me.* I just might have to give this new lady the benefit of the doubt.

We continue to walk. I realise instantly the new lady is now holding my lead. 'Jacob, would you like some more chicken?' I stop instantly, she is holding the tin and offering me another piece. I can't help the dribble oozing from my mouth. I look up into her big brown eyes and she smiles. I have a warm fuzzy feeling and don't know why. I sit nicely as she offers me more chicken. I try very hard not to snatch. Jane is smiling too. The new lady is still holding my lead as we walk and every time I try to pull her, she stops. We all stop. I want to walk and pull again. She stops. *This has confused me.* After around half an hour

I suddenly realise if I don't pull we don't stop and we get to walk further, a bit like my rescue lady did with me. She is grinning at me as she offers me more chicken. I think I just might like this new lady. She hands my lead back to Jane saying it has been a real pleasure and she has honestly enjoyed her time spent with us. I look up into her eyes. 'See you tomorrow Jacob and Jane, I have had a wonderful time,' she calls. *Me too,* I say to myself, still thinking of all the delicious chicken she has given me today.

Jane is very happy with me and is stroking me gently, telling me how proud she is. I feel like a king. I think I might like to see this new lady again tomorrow, if she turns up that is!

Jane is putting on my harness. 'Would you like to see Jo again today? *Who the heck is Jo?* We make our way outside and ahead I can see the lady from yesterday smiling at us. I think of chicken and wiggle my bum. I stop myself. I only do this for Jane and my rescue lady. I still need to be on my guard. 'Would you like some chicken Jacob?' she is asking. I watch as she pulls her magic tin out of her pocket. I wiggle my half tail again.

She is gently holding her hand out and I can't resist taking the chicken. Jane is giving her my lead. 'Have fun.' I instantly panic as Jane walks away. Jo is coaxing me forward. 'Come on handsome boy. We are going to have a nice walk and some chicken.' I glance back looking for Jane. She is not in sight. A piece of chicken suddenly lands in front of me. I hesitate but it smells too good and I cannot resist.

Jo talks to me a lot, she has such a calm, gentle and soothing voice. She lets me take my time and treats me as we go along. I do have to admit, I quite like her. Suddenly an hour has gone by. We have had a lovely time and we are on our way back to my house. Jane is waiting for us with a big smile on her face. I wiggle my half tail and bum frantically. Jo hands Jane my lead. 'See you tomorrow,' she calls as she walks away. I can't help myself and I bark at Jo. She turns around, looks at me and blows me a kiss. Suddenly, I am feeling very happy.

It is not long before Jane is taking me out again. She said Jo is bringing her partner with her. *I am not sure I want to share her with someone else.* Jo is waiting for me, suddenly I am wagging my half tail in excitement. She smiles. She has a lady with her who is a little smaller and has blue eyes and black hair. 'Hey Jacob, meet Becky. Becky meet Jacob the most handsome dog in the whole world.' Becky is smiling and reaching for her pocket. *I freeze* but instantly relax as she pulls out a magic tin exactly like the one Jo has. 'I hear you like chicken Jacob. Would you like some?' She throws a piece towards my shoulder. It's gone in a flash, I lick my lips gratefully. Jane has disappeared, and I didn't even notice. The two ladies chat and often stop so I can sniff.

Occasionally the magic tins appear, and I have allowed Jo to stroke me on my head and under my chin. I must admit I quite like the feeling I get when she strokes me, it makes me feel warm and fuzzy. We are sitting on the green grass in the sunshine. 'Didn't I tell you how gorgeous he is Becky?' 'He is truly handsome, I just love his character, his colour and his beautiful tail.' *Did I hear right? Becky loves my tail? They are not laughing at me like the others did?* They look at each other and nod. Jo speaks first. 'Jacob, how would you like to come and live with us? We will look after you and we promise to love you always. You will have two Mummies who will love, care and spoil you forever.' This has taken me completely by surprise. I like the fact they both have magic tins and have told me I will have my own warm, cosy bed, lots of toys, good food and loads of cuddles. The beautiful walks by the sea and on the Downs sound amazing too. I ponder, it's very tempting. I eagerly bark in agreement and wiggle my half tail, they smile at me, then at each other and we head back to my house. Jane seems thrilled when she hears the news that Jo and Becky want to take me home. 'We will see you tomorrow around one o'clock and we will have Jacob and his suitcase packed waiting for you.' Jo and Becky smile and both blow me a kiss. Jane doesn't stop chatting on the way back to my house, she's so excited 'Oh Jacob, I am so happy for you and we can keep in touch as you will be living just five miles away. How awesome is this?' I am feeling a little apprehensive. That evening I toss and turn in my sleep. *What will tomorrow bring? What if they change their mind? What if they don't show up?*

Chapter 11

* * *

I WAKE VERY EARLY panting rapidly. I haven't slept at all well. I kept having horrible flashbacks, but once I'd realised I'd only been dreaming, I started to relax as much as I possibly could. *Am I really leaving here today? Will I be safe or are they going to turn nasty on me once they have me in their home?* I am anxious, and I have wet myself. As if like magic Jane appears. 'Hey Jelly bum, what's the matter? Why haven't I got my morning bum wiggle?' I half attempt to move. *I really don't want to go anywhere. I want to stay here.* 'Jacob, I will be visiting you regularly to make sure you are happy. You trust me, don't you?' I instantly feel as if Jane has lifted a weight off my shoulders. I wiggle my bum. 'That's much more like it my Jelly bum,' she laughs.

'Right we need to pack up your toys and get ready for your Mums picking you up.' Your Mums have told me they have been shopping. You have two new beds, lots of toys and they have promised me you will be treated like the king you deserve to be.' *Wow, I wasn't expecting that!* I wish again that I could speak human. I look searchingly at Jane and with my eyes I try to say, *'I will try and make you very proud of me Jane. I love you and thank you from the bottom of my heart for everything you have done for me. I am going to miss you.'* I cannot help it as tears run down my face. *I know I need to be brave.*

My harness is on and my suitcase is packed, and we are on our way to see my two new Mums. They are waiting patiently in the car park by a silver car and as soon as they see us, both their faces light up with massive smiles. At this present moment, I am not too sure how I am feeling. They both walk towards us shaking their magic tins. I am going to get chicken and my bum starts to wiggle. 'Hey Jacob,' says Jo. 'Are you ready to come home with us?'

'Here is his suitcase, three days of wet and dry food and his toys and his blanket. His piggy is his favourite. I have already put his new identity tag with your details onto his collar. In a large envelope in the suitcase I have put his veterinary record, three month's complimentary veterinary insurance cover and his microchip details. You will need to change the ownership details of the microchip over to you as soon as you can. You will also find I have enclosed a voucher to get Jacob neutered free of charge when the time is appropriate. This is a very strict rule of ours and you will need to discuss this with your vet and inform us when it has been carried out. We always ask too that you continue with veterinary insurance.' 'Of course, Jane. We have already received insurance quotes from three different companies. I will change the microchip details over later today and I will register Jacob at our local vets,' replies Becky. Jo is putting my case onto the back seat of the car. She open's the boot. *I freeze* and start shaking. *I have never been able to tell anyone about the horrible incident with my tail.* Before I know it, Jane has scooped me up and I am in the boot of the car. The boot is shut, and I grimace. I can see Jane wiping her eyes and nose with a tissue. A tear rolls down my face once again. Becky is driving, and Jo is sitting on the back seat, so I can see her. The engine starts, and I can feel the familiar feeling of warm urine dripping down my leg. It isn't long until we come to a standstill. 'Welcome to your new home Jacob,' Jo whispers.

The boot is opening, and I cower waiting for the blow to hit my body. It doesn't happen. I slowly open my eyes. My two new Mum's are smiling down at me. 'Hey, don't worry Jacob, we all have accidents. Come on boy. Let's check out your new home.' *Am I dreaming? Is this really happening?* I jump out of the boot and my new Mum Jo leads me through a very large gate which my other new Mum Becky closes and bolts behind us. She is carrying my suitcase. Mum Jo opens another door and we are soon inside this nice house. It is lovely and warm and has a very homely feeling. It completely takes me by surprise, no dirty old vinyl in sight.

'Come on Jacob. We can't wait to show you around your new home.' Mum Jo has unclipped the lead from my harness and is now walking through another door. I follow slowly. *I still feel very nervous walking through door ways.* We are in a lovely square hallway. To the left I can see a warm and cosy looking bed. 'We hope you like your new bed Jay. I hope you don't mind me calling you Jay?' asks Mum Becky. *I bark in approval.* They both smile.

'Come on, shall we unpack your suitcase and you can check out the new toys we have bought you?' Mum Jo is asking me. *Is this real? Am I dreaming?* Two more doors open into a lounge and I can see another comfy bed. *Have they got another dog who lives here?* I can't see or smell one. 'This is your bed for daytime and the one in the hallway is for night time.' *Woof,* I bark in excitement. I can see so many toys lying by the bed. I edge closer to investigate.

Wow. A zebra, monkey, large fluffy ball, a giraffe who looks very similar to the one I destroyed, two teddy bears, tug toy and an elephant. *This is so cool.* Becky is unpacking my suitcase and is placing my toys next to my new ones. *My piggy!* I am so pleased to see him and jump on him. He oinks, and my two Mums laugh. I turn around. I can see a garden outside. I need to investigate. I rush towards the garden but come to an abrupt halt with a big bang. I am totally confused. I can hear my Mum's laughing, 'Silly billy, you can't run through glass windows. You probably haven't seen patio doors before, have you?' *Who is Billy? I can't see anyone.*

They continue to laugh. 'Shall we take you out into the garden? Maybe you need the toilet? Come on this way,' Mum Jo is saying as we walk back through the hallway and out through another door. I cower once again at the door. Mum Jo is watching me closely. 'Hey, the door isn't going to hurt you, I promise.' I have never been in a garden like this before. I look around in amazement.

High fences surround my new house and I can see a very large area of green grass. Awesome. I run onto the grass, instantly stopping as soon as my paws touch down. *This is very weird.* It looks like real grass butt doesn't feel like grass? *What is going on?* Seeing my confused look Mum Jo laughs. 'This is called Astroturf, don't worry, you can wee and poo on it. It is very easy to clean, and it never needs mowing. It saves us so much time and it's nicer for you Jacob.' I take a few steps. It feels bouncy. I am certainly going to enjoy running around on this new surface. I can see a few flower pots and a small border with some bushes and trees. My nose is directing me towards the border. I sniff. I pee. I sniff. I pee! 'Good toilet,' says Mum Jo beaming with delight.

'Come on Jay,' calls Mum Becky. 'Let's go back inside and get you a drink of water.' I follow her as quick as I can. *Slurp, slurp, slurp.* Lovely fresh clean water. I follow her into a big kitchen and watch as she puts a kettle on to boil. I jump up on the surfaces to have a nosey. 'Off,' she gently says. I get down when Mum Jo walks in. 'I need to do some work. I will be in the office if you need me.'

Oh no, I don't want her going to work. I want her to stay here with me. I wait for her to go out the front door, but she doesn't. She opens another door. I see a desk, chair and a lot of computer equipment. 'This is my office Jacob. I work from home. During the day time it will be just you and me as Mum Becky works in an office in Town.' *Am I hearing this right? I am not going to be shut away and left on my own, you're really going to stay with me here?*

Mum Jo is sitting at her computer wearing this funny head set. She is talking to herself. *How strange. I wonder where Mum Becky has got to?* I investigate the rooms downstairs but can't find her. I double check the kitchen. No-one is watching me, so I have an opportunity to have a quick sniff around. I still can't find any crumbs, but I can see a tea towel hanging off the drawer. *If I pull that, maybe some crumbs will appear?* Nothing. I pick up the tea towel and throw it in the air. Great catch. I do it again but miss catching it and turn to see Mum Becky standing watching me. I instantly cower against the cupboard. 'Oh Jay, please don't cower. You can play with everything, even if it is with our best tea towel. It makes me sad to see you cower like that. This is your home forever. We are never going to hurt you, I promise. Would you like some chicken?'. She opens a cupboard and pulls out some chicken. She is holding some out on the palm of her hand. I can't resist and take it as gently as I can. She starts to stroke me gently. 'Come on let us go and find Mum Jo and maybe we can all go for a walk, it will give you chance to check out your new neighbourhood.' I follow her to the office. 'Hey, shall we take Jay for a walk?' she is asking Mum Jo. 'Two seconds and I will be with you.'

Chapter 12

* * *

MUM JO HAS BROUGHT me a new harness. 'Jacob, this is called a Perfect Fit Harness. I reckon purple is going to look absolutely fabulous on you.' My new harness feels soft and comfy against my body. She takes it on and off four times. I watch closely as she adjusts four clips until she seems ecstatic that it is a snug fit against my body. She clips one end of the new lead onto a ring on my chest and the other end onto the ring on my back. I have never seen a harness or a lead like this before. 'Wow, how handsome do you look Jacob?' Mum Jo is asking me, looking very proud. I am so relieved I don't have to have anything attached to my collar anymore. I shiver at the thought of the pain it used to cause my neck and throat.

'How about you take Jacob's lead and I walk by your side?' she is asking Mum Becky. 'That would be great,' she replies. Off we go. I am still not over happy about going through the doors, but I try to be as brave as I can. We walk up a driveway, my nose is high in the air, there hundreds of different smells coming at me from all directions. I can see houses ahead and soon we are at the top and start walking to the right. Something whizzes past and frightens the life out of me. Mum Becky is taken by surprise as I start to run and drag her behind me. A car is now whizzing towards me. I need to protect my new Mums and lunge at it as fast as I can with my teeth. By now, Mum Jo has my lead and is talking to me calmly. Mum Becky is breathing heavily and has her hands on her hips bent over. 'I bet you haven't seen too many cars or walked on too many roads by the look of it, have you?' *Why does Mum Jo seem to understand dog language? Is she a mind reader?*

'Come on, let's get you home. I will come up with a plan to help you,' Mum Jo is now holding my lead and gently pulling on the end which is attached to my chest. I have no choice but to walk nicely beside her. Mum Becky is following behind. 'I wasn't expecting that. Why does he want to chase and attack cars? That's a bit silly.' 'He is a collie Becky and sometimes their natural instincts are to chase cars or anything that moves,' Mum Jo responds. 'Oh,' was Mum Becky's reply. We are back inside my new house and I realise I am feeling very tired. 'Why don't you have a lie down Jacob, whilst we sort out some dinner?'

This sounds a great idea. I paw at my new bed and collapse into a heap. I can hear my two Mums chatting in the kitchen. I close my eyes. I awake with a start. *Beep, beep, beep.* I bolt up and run towards the noise and bark. *I hate this noise.* I am panting and barking. 'Becky turn the microwave off quickly.' Becky does as Mum Jo asks. *That's better.* I take deep breaths. 'Ok, so you don't like the microwave. I wonder why? Never mind we will use the oven instead.' Mum Becky is looking confused. I wish I could talk human and tell them why I don't like microwaves. I hate these flashbacks I have. *Will I always have them?*

Mum Jo is sitting on the floor next to me giving me some chicken and stroking me. I feel happy again. *I can smell eggs.* 'Hey Jay, you are having boiled eggs, chopped carrot, broccoli and a few garden peas with a little bit of the food you are used to. Is that ok?' Mum Jo asks. *Is this ok? It is more than ok, totally awesome in fact*, I think to myself grinning. When my dinner is ready Mum Becky carries it into the hallway and places it next to my water bowl. I sit and wait patiently, just as Jane had taught me. She said it was good manners. Mum Becky is smiling. 'Good boy Jay, eat it all up.' Wow, this is a truly, luxurious dinner. I cannot believe my luck. I lick the bowl clean and double check to make sure I haven't left any. I have a nice long drink of fresh water. My Mum's are sitting at the table in the kitchen eating their dinner. 'Was that nice Jay?' Mum Becky asks. *I respond with a woof.* I walk closer and try and sniff as near as I can to their dinner. 'Jacob, lay down please. You have had your dinner. We are having ours.' I lay down on the floor letting out a big grunt and they both laugh.

They have finished their food and are washing the dishes. They even wash my food bowl! I cannot believe how clean this kitchen is. Not a crumb in sight. I follow them into the lounge. I turn to see this large square thing sitting on a very large cabinet. It is flashing images and talking loudly. I move as close as I dare to and bark.

'Hey, surely you have seen a television before Jacob? Maybe you haven't. Hold on I will turn the volume down for you,' Mum Jo says. 'I know what. I will get you an antler.' I honestly haven't a clue what she is talking about as I follow her into the kitchen. She is opening a cupboard and I can smell something very nice. She is offering it to me. 'Here you are this is an antler for you to chew.' I take it from her hand holding it tightly in my mouth and follow her back to the lounge. She is sitting next to Mum Becky on a sofa. I lay down and start chomping. It is nice to have something to chew on at last. My gums hurt, and Jane had told them I am teething.

'Come on Jacob, time to go to the toilet and then bed for us all. You have had such a long day and you must be shattered. Let's go, I will come with you,' says Mum Jo. I follow her closely and we head out into the garden. She sits down on a step and patiently waits whilst I sniff around and pee. I need a poo too but what if it bounces? I haven't done one on this spongy surface yet. I circle and circle. *This is the spot.* Mum Jo is smiling. 'Good toilet Jacob. I am so proud of you.' *I feel like a king but don't understand why humans get so excited when I do a toilet?*

She turns to walk inside but I am not ready for bed. I want to play. I nip her ankle with my teeth and instantly regret it. 'We will have none of that nonsense Jacob. Come on, time for bed.'

Suddenly I feel tired, bed sounds like a good idea. I don't want to get into too much trouble on my first day as I quite like it here. Mum Becky has filled up my water bowl and has turned most of the lights off. I try and follow Mum Jo up the stairs, but she has shut a gate behind her. 'Off to bed Jacob, you will find a tasty treat on your bed. Night, night, baby boy. I love you.' *I cannot believe what I just heard.* I try hard to stop a single tear from rolling down my face. No-one has ever told me they love me apart from my real Mum. The other light is turned off and I walk towards my bed. I find the treat, eat it and settle down. I feel so happy and relaxed, within seconds my eyes are closing. I sigh peacefully and drift off to sleep.

Chapter 13

* * *

I CAN'T REMEMBER waking up in the night. I open my eyes and realise I hadn't been dreaming at all, I am in my new home, and this is real. I hear a movement coming from upstairs, so jump out of bed as quick as I can and walk towards the gate. I can see Mum Jo looking over the bannister at me smiling. My half a tail is wagging as fast as it can possibly go. She walks down the stairs towards me. 'Good morning, Jacob. I hope you slept well. You are such a good boy. Come on, I will take you out to see if you need the toilet.' Ten minutes later and we are back inside. Mum Becky seems to be rushing around. 'I will get a cuppa on the way,' she is calling to Mum Jo. She stops as she sees me. 'Hey Jay, what a brilliant boy you were last night. We are so proud of you. I need to go to work now. I will come for a walk with you when I get home. See you later.' She has disappeared out of the front door.

Mum Jo is making herself a drink and getting my breakfast. I cannot believe how nice and peaceful it is here. I can even hear birds chirping happily in the garden. I cannot get my head around this at all, *maybe I am still dreaming?* After a lovely breakfast and another trip to the garden, Mum Jo is sitting in her office with those headphones on again talking to herself. I bark, she turns and puts one finger up to her lips. I bark again, and she does the same. I eventually understand what she is asking of me as this is exactly what the lady next door at my old house used to do. Time for me to go off and investigate. The gate on the stairs is open. I slowly climb the stairs as quietly as possible. I can see a very large bed to the left through an open door. I jump onto it. It takes me by surprise, it feels so bouncy. I stop and look around. I can even see out of the window but for some reason the garden looks a very long way away.

    I jump down and see a sock on the floor. I pick it up and throw it around. I carry it into the next room. I stop in amazement. Can you believe I am looking at the biggest water bowl I have ever seen in the whole of my life? There is not much water in it though, so I jump up, lean forward and stick my head as far as I can into the bottom of this huge bowl. I open my mouth. I have completely forgotten I am carrying my sock. I watch it as it floats around. I lean as far forward as I can and for one moment I nearly fall head first into the bottom. *Wow, this must have been designed for a very huge dog.* After two attempts, at last I retrieve my sock. It is dripping with water. I shake it around in my mouth as fast as I can to try and dry it. Splashes of water are flying everywhere.

I suddenly stand still. I am sure I can hear Mum Jo. 'Jacob, are you ok? Where are you?' I run to the top of the stairs wagging my half a tail proudly with the wet sock which is dripping with water. Mum Jo has a shocked look on her face for a moment and then smiles. 'That's Mum Becky's fault for not shutting the gate before she went to work. Come on, down you come.' I immediately oblige and within two seconds I am at the bottom. She is looking directly at me. 'Jacob, please can you drop my sock?', she asks nicely. I dive passed her running into the lounge. I love this game! Mum Jo is following me. She is asking me again to drop her sock. I run passed her again like lighting straight into the kitchen. This is great fun. I crawl under the table. 'Jacob how about you swap the sock for some chicken?' I can see her sitting on the floor with her magic tin. I crawl out from under the table leaving my sock behind. 'Good boy, Jacob,' she is saying as I take the chicken. She is getting up and I can see the perfect opportunity, I dive under the table, grab my sock and run back into the lounge. 'Oh, I see, you think this is a game, don't you?' She is walking to the hallway, dropping pieces of chicken on the floor. I cannot resist. I rush over and gobble it all up in a flash. I turn around to see Mum Jo standing holding my sock with a very big smile on her face. *Oh well, game over.* Mum Jo heads towards her office. 'I have some work to finish off and then we will go for a walk. Is that ok Jay?' *Woof!* I reply.

Ten minutes later we are on our way up the drive. We reach the top and out of nowhere somethings whizzes past me at great speed just like yesterday. I turn to chase whatever it was, but Mum Jo has my lead tightly in her grasp. 'Come on, we are walking this way, it's only a car Jay.' The lead on the front of my chest is stopping me from going too far from Mum Jo. I can see another car whizzing towards us. Mum Jo is standing still. 'Watch

Jacob.' My body is shaking with anticipation but it has gone by in a flash. 'Good boy, Jacob. See it wasn't going to hurt you.' Her magic tin appears, I snatch the chicken from her hand. I am feeling anxious. Mum Jo lets out a long deep breath. We walk a few steps further and arrive at this square looking thing with a seat inside it. Mum Jo sits down. 'We are going to sit here and watch the cars go by Jacob. I will tell you the make of them and if you are a good boy, I will give you chicken.'

I am so focussed on her magic tin, I am too late to respond as another car zoom's past. I had missed it. 'Vauxhall Astra,' she is saying as she gives me a piece of chicken. I am watching the tin. I can hear another car fly by. 'Audi,' she says as I get a piece of chicken. 'Mini Cooper.' I get more chicken. I can hear the cars, but I want the chicken more. Mercedes. Alfa Romeo. Jeep. BMW. Citroen. Ford Fiesta. Citroen. Peugeot. Renault. Mazda. Volkswagen. *I never knew there were so many breeds of car.*

'Good boy Jacob, that will do for today. You did very well, and I am very proud of you. Come on let's go home.' We turn. Another car whizzes past. 'Watch.' She is holding a piece of chicken between her eyes. I am totally focussed on her eyes. Another car whizzes by. I don't move I want the chicken. 'Good boy, you are so clever.' I get my chicken and within minutes we are back in the safety of my home.

I have a very long drink and feel totally exhausted. I lay down in the lounge, the sun is shining through the windows. Mum Jo is up to something. I can hear her putting something into a plug hole, I remember this sound. I lift my head and see this noisy machine moving up and down the hallway. I have seen something like this before at my other Mum's house. I need to get it away from Mum Jo in case it hurts her. I launch myself and grab the front of the machine as firmly as I can, tugging it away from Mum Jo to the best of my ability. Mum Jo looks shocked and suddenly the noise stops. 'Jacob, don't be silly, it is just a vacuum cleaner.' The noise starts again. I can't see the front as it is going the other way. I jump as high as I can and grab the wire pulling it around in my mouth. The noise stops. 'Hey, Jacob. The vacuum cleaner is not going to hurt you. I will prove it to you.' She unplugs the machine and moves it next to my bed. I look at it in disgust. *How dare she park it next to my bed!*

'Go and lay down for a while Jacob. I will get you your antler and you can relax in the lounge.' *This is the life*, I think as I lay in the sun chewing my antler.

Click, click, click, click, click, click. I jump up. I am on high alert. I listen. *Click, click, click, click, click, click.* I run to where the noise is coming from. It is coming from inside Mums office. She has her headphones on. I look up. *Click, click, click, click, click, click.* There is a black square box spitting out large sheets of white paper. The paper is heading towards my Mum. *Oh no you don't.* I jump as high as I can and grab the paper biting it and shaking it as hard as I can. Mum is taken completely unaware and is looking at me with her mouth wide open. *I think she looks worried.* I jump up again. This time I grab the black thing, I can't grasp it, it's too big. I keep trying. My Mum has taken her headphones off and the clicking has stopped.

'Oh Jacob, what are you doing? I was just printing out some important work.' *Is she angry with me?* I can feel urine running down my leg. 'Oh, Jacob darling, come here. I am not angry with you. I need to remember that you may have not heard or seen so many different things before and it is my job as your Mum to prove to you they are not going to hurt you.' She is stroking me gently. *I really am sorry. I cannot help it.* I watch as Mum Jo cleans it up. *She never gets angry with me?*

I can hear the front door opening and freeze. It's only Mum Becky arriving home from work. I wiggle my bum in excitement. 'Hey Jay, have you been ok? Have you had a fun day?' *Woof*, I say. I will go and get changed and we can take you out onto the Downs?' *Woof.* 'Hi Jo,' she calls as she runs up the stairs. She has forgotten to shut the gate again. Off I go bounding up the stairs after her. 'Sorry Jo, my fault he is up here. I left the gate open.' 'Yep, you left it open earlier,' Mum Jo is calling back. 'Long story, I will tell you later.'

Chapter 14

* * *

WE ARE READY TO GO. I expected to be heading up the driveway but both Mum's stop next to the car. I immediately start to shake, and my legs feel wobbly. The boot of the car is open. Mum Jo is looking at me with a concerned look. 'Come on Jacob, we are going for a lovely walk on the Downs. Can you jump in?' I stay rigid and still. Before I know what is happening she has scooped me up and placed me in the boot and gently closed the door.' I can't help it, I have wet myself again. We are only in the car for a few minutes but already I am panting and anxious. We stop, and the boot opens. 'Poor Jay, look at the state you have got yourself into,' Mum Becky is saying. I can see her looking at the wet bed, but she just continues talking. 'It is a good job I have some water for you, you look very thirsty.' Mum Jo carefully lifts me out and places me onto a gravelled floor. I think we are in a car park and I watch as Mum Becky pours water into my bowl. I do need a drink and within seconds I have drunk it all. I feel a lot better now. Mum Jo is taking the wet towel out and is putting a fresh towel into the boot. I watch as she attaches an extra-long lead onto the back of my harness. 'Believe it or not Jacob, this a lunge line normally used for horses. I thought it would be ideal for our long walks as it will give you some freedom whilst we work on your recall. I love the vibrant colour, it blends in so nicely with your Perfect Fit Harness. You have to be colour coordinated, don't you?' *What a wonderful walk we had.* We were out for nearly two hours and I was in my element. So many areas to sniff and mark. We bumped into a few different people with their dogs. Each time I'd sat quietly and was very well behaved. I was totally focussed on the chicken Mum Jo was holding between her eyes. I wasn't at all bothered about anything else going on around me.

    I let myself down on the journey home by wetting myself again. My Mums never get angry with me. *I don't understand?* I had a lovely dinner followed by cuddles with my Mums and soon it was bed time again. Mum Becky took me out for toilet in the garden and on the way in I was a bit naughty. I was feeling mischievous and as she started to run, I nipped her ankle. I didn't mean to and I immediately licked her to say I was sorry. *I only wanted to play.*

The vacuum cleaner is still next to my bed. Mum Jo is keeps placing treats on it. I am shocked. They are my treats and as soon as I can, I snatch them off his head and eat them. I laugh to myself, *serves him right*. There is no way I am prepared to share my treats with him.

It is soon morning again and Mum Becky has just gone off to work, in a rush as usual. I follow Mum Jo out into the garden. I keep an eye on her as she opens the door to the shed, I have never been inside here before. It is crammed full of different objects and I can see a bicycle in the corner. Mum Jo is having a good rummage around and eventually picks up some plastic plates, a piece of wood and a little square case. I follow her back up the garden path. She stops, sits on a step, opens the case, puts a plastic plate on top of the piece of wood and with this little machine drills one single hole into it. She continues to do the same to each of the plastic plates. *How weird.* I am intrigued as to what she is up to.

I watch closely as she carries the plates into the kitchen with me following behind closely. She opens a cupboard and pulls out a big ball of string. I watch as she threads a long piece of string through each hole. 'Jacob, I am going to try something. I think it will help you.' She is now looking inside the fridge and pulls out a tube of something and a jar. Now she is getting a knife from the kitchen drawer. 'Wait here, I will be back in a second,' she says heading towards the front door. I sit and wait patiently for her to come back in, my head tilting to the left and the right. I can hear different noises coming from outside, I really haven't a clue what she is up to. Within minutes she is back but isn't carrying anything.

'Come on let's go for a walk.' My harness is on and I can't help drooling as I watch her fill my magic tin with chicken. I had assumed we were going up the driveway, but I freeze when I see the boot of the car is open. Before I know it, she has lifted me in. I can smell cheese and peanut butter. The car is now filled with the aroma of lovely smelling food. She is sitting on the edge of the boot with me and is pointing to the dog guard.

'Look, there they are, the plastic plates.' I can see they are tied onto my guard.

My nose is working overtime. *Can you believe the cheese and peanut butter smell is coming from the plates?* 'Go on Jacob, they are yours. Look you can lick them.' *This is great.* I look at her and turn around and tuck in. I had forgotten I am still in the boot of the car.

Once I have licked the plates clean, Mum Jo lifts me out and is telling me what a good boy I am. This is the first time I have been in a car without wetting myself. *I am feeling very proud.*

Chapter 15

✳ ✳ ✳

MY FIRST THREE WEEKS in my new home have flown by. We have a good daily routine. When Mum Becky has gone to work, I have my breakfast and during the morning Mum Jo continues to take me out and we sit at the bus stop naming cars and eating chicken. I am feeling less bothered by the cars whizzing by. I trust my Mums, they are not scared so why should I be? Mum Jo seems very pleased with me. I love her with every ounce of my heart.

When Mum Becky arrives home late afternoon from work, she usually gets changed and we head off for a long walk. We normally go out in the car and I am proud to tell you I have only wet myself twice in the last fifteen days. I always have cheese and peanut butter on my plastic plates and I still lick them anxiously whilst the car is moving. Mum Jo says it is giving my brain something to focus on. Mum Jo always carries the tubs in the car and if I have cleared my plates on the way to the walk, she refills them for the return journey home.

Sometimes Mum Jo and me just sit in the boot of the car chatting. I like this as this is our special time. I still sleep next to that vacuum cleaner, but I always manage to eat his treats before he can. He has been very, very quiet lately.

Mum Jo has now put a gate on her office door. I can see her but can't go in there. She is crafty as sometimes she throws me treats into the hallway just as I can hear, click, click, click. I try and ignore the machine which is apparently called a printer. I quickly eat my treats and to be honest the noise has usually stopped by the time I have finished eating them.

Mum Jo has been acting a little weird the last couple of days. She keeps pushing the vacuum cleaner around the house. *No sound and no noise?*

I absolutely adore the *'watch'* game we play daily. I sit, and Mum Jo puts a treat between her eyes and says 'watch.' Once I am totally focussed on her eyes I get the treat. I love the connection I feel when I stare into Mum Jo's big brown eyes. My heart always skips a beat.

I have learned to give my left and right paw when asked. I can lay down on command. If I bark too much my

Mums put one finger to their lips and I know I need to be quiet. I also love to chase a tennis ball. Mum throws, I fetch. I drop. Mum throws and we play and play and play.

Another favourite game of mine is when my Mum's ask me to sit and wait in a room in the house.

Today, Mum Jo, asks me to sit and wait in the kitchen. My ears are moving back and forth. I hear them moving around upstairs. I sit and wait patiently, I hear Mum Becky call, 'Jacob come and find us.' I run around the house searching using my nose to sniff them out. I have found Mum Becky under the bed. I cannot find Mum Jo. *Where is she?* I run back up the stairs, back down the stairs. I check every room. I stand still. I hear a giggle. It is coming from the bathroom. I check again but no one is there. *Maybe she has fallen down the big water bowl?* I stop, I can hear her giggle again. I can smell her. I know she is not too far away but where is she? I turn just in time to see Mum Jo jumping out of the bath 'Boo,' she shouts out loudly. I jump backwards, she is laughing hysterically. *Woof*, I laugh back.

One day, Mum Jo hid inside a wardrobe. It took me ages to find her. We have so much fun together. There isn't a day that goes by without my two Mum's telling me how much they love me. They know I feel the same, I let them know in my own way. My life is now complete and happy.

Chapter 16

✳ ✳ ✳

I AM WATCHING MUM JO, she is walking around with the vacuum cleaner again. She is pulling something out of his body. It looks like a trunk. I watch in disbelief as the vacuum cleaner's trunk pushes my favourite tennis ball towards me. I pick up my ball and take it back to mum Jo. The trunk continues to push my ball and I return it back to Mum Jo. We continue to play like this for quite a while. What happens next takes me completely by surprise. The hoover is now making a noise but I have my eyes on the trunk. My tennis ball is stuck on the end of the trunk. I watch as the trunk rises high into the air and throws my ball towards me. I jump up and catch the ball in my mouth. *Wow, what a clever trunk.* I take my ball back and the trunk plays with me again. I cannot believe my sleeping partner the vacuum cleaner has been keeping this a secret for all this time. I wish I had known before as I would have made friends with him sooner. I look up and see a big smile on Mum Jo's face.

It is now November. Most of the leaves have fallen off the trees in our garden and Mum Jo has been working hard to clear them up. 'You want to help me clear the garden Jacob?', she asks. *Here we go again.* Mum Jo goes to the shed and pulls out the hosepipe. She turns it on to full power and blasts the leaves across the garden into the corner by the fence. My tennis ball is usually hiding in the middle of the pile of leaves. My job is to find and retrieve it. I love this game. I drop my ball at Mum Jo's feet, and the water coming out of the hosepipe moves my ball around the garden. I try to get it without getting too wet but by the time we are usually finished I am totally soaked and so is Mum Jo. I shake the whole of my body close to Mum Jo showering her even more. It always makes her laugh.

Today is the first of December. Mum Becky is excited as she keeps telling me it will soon be Christmas. She keeps pleading with Mum Jo, 'Can I put the Christmas tree up today?' 'Not yet,' Mum Jo keeps telling her. I really haven't a clue what they are talking about.

What is a Christmas tree? 'Jo, please can we put the tree up today, Mum Becky pleads. It is Jacob's first Christmas and I want him to share in the True Christmas Spirit.' 'Oh Becky, you certainly know how to make me feel guilty. If you must,' she lets out a huge sigh. Mum Becky is jumping up and down singing, 'Rudolph the red nosed reindeer had a very shiny nose.' *Who is Rudolph?* I ask myself puzzled.

Mum Becky is running up the stairs at a great speed. Thankfully she has forgotten to close the gate again, so I run closely behind. She is opening the bedroom door and has disappeared into the wardrobe. I am intrigued and pop my head in to have a look. I can see her crawling through another door at the back of the wardrobe. *Bang, bang, bang.* Now she is trying to crawl back out of this tiny square door and is looking completely frazzled. I rush towards her and plant a very big slobbery lick across her face. She laughs. She is dragging a large bag and box behind her and is crawling on all fours and to me she looks like she is pretending to be a dog. Eventually she stands up straight but is grunting and puffing. 'I have found a big bag full of delights and I more importantly I have the Christmas tree.'

Down the stairs she goes dragging the items behind her. I watch in amusement. *Whatever is going on?* I sit on my bed in the hallway. From here I can see Mum Jo working away and talking to herself as usual and Mum Becky is putting up a tree in the lounge? To be honest, I think she has really lost the plot this time. I watch as she spends ages putting funny objects and shiny balls onto the branches. *Why is she hanging balls on the tree?* She is very excited and eventually calls in Mum Jo. 'Look at the tree Jo, I hope the lights work. Close your eyes and I will turn them on.' A few seconds later, lights are flickering all over the tree. I rush across to her, my half a tail wagging in excitement.

Suddenly a few of the objects are flying off the tree and rolling around on the lounge carpet. I rush to retrieve one of the baubles. It is very hard to keep hold of. It keeps slipping around in my mouth. It tastes weird too. 'On no, Jacob, please drop my bauble,' Mum Becky is asking. I stand and stare at her full of mischief. Mum Jo has noticed

I am getting ready to run off with the bauble and pulls out her magic tin. 'Jacob drop.' I immediately rush across to her. She takes out a piece of chicken.' I drop the bauble. Mum Becky looks relieved. She quickly picks it up and hangs it back onto a branch. They look at each other and laugh a fully blown belly laugh. I woof in reply, I am laughing too.

Chapter 17

✻ ✻ ✻

MUM JO IS LETTING ME out for my morning toilet. 'It is snowing Jacob, how exciting,' she is saying as she puts on her coat and boots. *What is she talking about?* I watch as she opens the back door. I put one foot on the step and come to a complete stop. *Wow, everything is white.* What is all this white fluffy stuff flying around? I hesitate. Mum Jo is calling me a wuss! She is going out first. I stay still for a few seconds. I can't see her, I need to check she is safe. I reluctantly put my paws on the white stuff. It feels cold and soft. The white stuff is falling on top of me and flying around. It reminds me of when I tried to help my teddy bear, but this white stuff disappears on me and it feels wet.

Mum Jo is calling me. I run to catch her up. I love the feel of this white stuff. Even the bushes are white. Mum Jo is picking up some of the snow and is making it into a ball. *Wow, how clever is this?* I watch. 'Are you ready to catch Jacob?' *Woof!* She is throwing the ball straight towards me. I dive to the left and catch it. It is dissolving in my mouth and tastes like water. *Where has my ball gone?* Mum Jo is laughing like a crazy woman. We play for ages until we are totally worn out and head back inside. Mum Jo dries me off with a big soft towel.

Later that afternoon when Mum Becky arrived home from work, we all went out to play in the garden. They kept making balls out of the snow and throwing them at each other. I love hearing them laugh. The next morning the snow had disappeared. Everything was just wet. *Where had it gone?*

'It is Christmas Day tomorrow. Father Christmas is coming tonight. He is going to leave lots of presents under the tree Jacob,' Mum Becky is telling me. *Who is this Father Christmas?* I can assure you now, I will not be letting anyone into our house. Later that evening when Mum Becky had gone to bed I watched as Mum Jo popped into her office. She came out with a very large bag and gently placed loads and loads of presents under the branches of the tree. 'Tonight, you don't need to be on guard Jacob,' she says smiling. *I woof* in response but before long I drift off to sleep.

'Merry 1ˢᵗ Christmas Jay,' Mum Becky is calling from upstairs. I jump up and woof back. Mum Jo is now rushing down the stairs. 'Let's get the kettle on and we can have a look and see what Father Christmas has left for you.' *Now I am really confused.* I am one hundred per cent sure no-one came into our house last night. 'Come on Jacob, off you go out to the toilet and when you come back in we can open our presents.'

We sit in the lounge. Mum Becky has put all the presents that had been sitting under the tree into three different piles. 'That is your pile Jay,' she says as she points to this enormous pile of presents. *Yippee.* My Mums start opening their presents and suddenly paper is flying everywhere. This is great fun. I rush to help them pull the paper off. The delight on their faces is priceless. 'Come on Jacob, open yours.' Mum Jo is holding out one of my presents. She is holding one end and I have the other. We pull and tug until all the paper is off. This is totally awesome. Present after present is revealed. I have a squeaky Father Christmas, squeaky fluffy snow man, reindeer, penguin, cuddly elephant, three puzzle games, a ball that makes all different animal noises when I push it, a big bag of tennis balls, three tug toys and lots of bags of treats.

Even though I didn't see Father Christmas I really do like him. Paper is scattered all around the lounge and my Mums seem very happy with their gifts. I look around and smile. *I love my family, how lucky am I?*

It is now the afternoon and we have been out for a wonderful long walk. I can smell chicken cooking and my Mum's are busy preparing dinner. 'Jay you are going to have your first Christmas dinner. Chicken, carrots, peas, broccoli, mashed potato, Yorkshire pudding and gravy. How does this sound?' Mum Becky is asking. *Woof,* I reply greedily. We all have our dinner at the same time. My Mums are wearing paper hats and laughing as they eat. I absolutely love my Christmas dinner. It is the best dinner I have ever had. *I wonder how often Christmas is?* What a fabulous day today has been. I am lying on my bed. My tummy is full to bursting. I glance around looking at my new, wonderful toys. I can see my Mum's laying on the sofa fast asleep. I feel content, my eyes are heavy and within seconds I am fast asleep too.

Chapter 18

* * *

IT IS NOW THE FIRST WEEK of February. Last Sunday we went to a local dog show. I was slightly concerned when I heard Mum Becky say she was going to enter me in the waggiest tail competition? I really didn't want people laughing at me. Mum Becky had her magic tin with her. 'We love your tail Jay, it is part of your character. Anyway, I have always wanted to enter a class at a dog show, humour me please,' she had said. I'd looked around in amazement. So many different looking dogs. One was as small as a rabbit and to my astonishment another one was the size of a pony!

There were thirty-two entries in total. It seemed like we were hanging around for ages. I watched as two women walked towards each dog. They would spend a couple of minutes holding a treat to see if the dog wagged their tail. I laughed to myself as the dog the size of a pony had fallen asleep and had completely refused to get up. He didn't even get his treat.

Three more to go and then my turn. 'Ok, when I say, hey Jay who has the waggiest tail in the whole wide world, you wiggle your bottom as fast as you can,' Mum Becky had told me. The two women were talking to the dog and owner next to us, but he kept barking at the treat and sitting down. They couldn't even see his tail. *How silly is he?*

Then came my turn. The two ladies asked Mum Becky my name. At that precise moment I saw Mum Jo walking towards me. My bottom and tail were wagging at a furious speed. I heard one of the ladies say, 'Wow, what a fantastic wiggly tail and bum you have Jacob.' I had taken my treat gently from them and they moved on to the next dog. My Mums were delighted with me. Ten minutes later a loud voice started calling people into the centre of the ring. I was half listening. The loud voice spoke again. 'And in second place, we have Jacob.' I could hear Mum Jo shouting 'Well done our baby boy.' Mum Becky was proudly walking towards the middle of the ring with me at her side. 'Jay, Jay, what a brilliant and clever boy you are. I love you so much.' She had pulled out a tissue and wiped her eyes. I had never seen tears of happiness, the only tears I had seen before, were always ones of sadness. One of the two ladies had congratulated us and presented me with a very large blue rosette, a container of treats and a small silver cup. As we left the ring, I couldn't believe it. So many people were clapping and cheering at ME. This had to be the proudest moment of my life. Mum Jo was waiting for us. She was on her knees cuddling me, telling me how proud she was. I even got to try my very first doggy ice cream as a well-done treat. *And to think I had been worried about people laughing at my tail?*

Once we arrived home, my Mums informed me we were going to celebrate. I had posed with my rosette, trophy and treats whilst they took what seemed like hundreds of photographs. Mum Becky was so excited and couldn't wait to put them on Facebook, whatever that is.

I had a very special dinner that evening. Mum Becky had celebrated by drinking a beer, then another and another. Eventually there were no beers left and an empty box sat on the kitchen floor. I walked into the kitchen and put my head into the bottom of the box to have a sniff and investigate. Somehow my head had managed to get stuck. I'd lifted my head up and tried to walk to find my Mums, but I couldn't see a thing. I shook my head to the left and to the right as hard as I could. The box wouldn't budge. Bang. I walked into a cupboard. I could hear Mum Jo calling me. 'Jacob, where are you?' The next moment, I could hear hysterical laughter. 'Becky, get your iPhone quickly,' Mum Jo was calling. A few seconds later the box was removed off my head. 'Oh Jacob, you are so funny. I haven't laughed so much in ages. I cannot believe you were walking around with a box on your head. You do make us laugh,' and with that Mum Jo had planted a big kiss on my face.

I need to tell you some very exciting news. I don't need plastic plates on my dog guard anymore. I haven't peed in the car for over two months. To be honest I love going out in the car, we always go somewhere beautiful and have such wonderful walks. I absolutely adore going to the beach and I have even paddled in the sea. I have also visited the local pub a few times with my Mum's and their friends for a meal and a drink. *How cool is this?*

My Mum's have told me it is my 1st birthday tomorrow. Apparently, I will be having lots of presents and I will also be having a big surprise as two special visitors who will be popping in to see me. *I wonder who they will be?*

Chapter 19

* * *

TODAY IS THE 14TH FEBRUARY. 'Happy birthday to you, Happy birthday to you, happy 1st birthday darling Jacob, Happy birthday to you.' I look at my dog shaped birthday cake. It smells delicious. A single candle sits glowing. I look up to see both my Mums smiling down at me. Pure love is shining through their eyes. Their faces are full of happiness. I *woof,* in delight. *What a year it has been.*

THE MOTTO OF THIS STORY:
NEVER GIVE UP ON A RESCUE DOG LIKE JACOB
HE WILL REPAY YOUR LOVE AND KINDNESS TENFOLD

♥

A POEM

By Michelle Holland

FROM MY HEART

You were badly treated, abused and smacked
Essential food and water you lacked
You had just half a tail, we will never know why
Each time I think of this, I want to cry

You had so many problems for us to address
You were certainly a challenge, I will confess
You had suffered horribly until rescued and secure
It was truly horrific, what you had to endure

I walked you daily, you pulled hard and strong
You just didn't know, what was right or wrong
On the 23rd August we brought you home
Where you would be safe and free to roam

You have a wiggly bum that brightens my day
You are cheeky and loving and are here to stay
Deep down inside, you were just misunderstood
You just needed guidance to be my best bud

You hated the hoover, the printer you'd attack
Maybe some people would have taken you back
You hated the microwave, you would get in a state
We were meant to be together, most definitely fate

I never gave up, as I knew deep inside
You were a loving dog who would stay by my side
So loyal, so loving, you have come a long way
You are relaxed and happy and love to play.

It takes time and patience and lots of love
Eventually it all fits, like a perfect glove
You have learnt to trust with the big steps you've taken
Even when bruised, scared and shaken

We have a special connection, we have so much fun
You pinch the tea towels and love to run
Thank you, dear Jacob, I will never regret
The day I first saw you, the first day we met.

All my love, Mum Jo
xxxxxx

♥

Printed in Great Britain
by Amazon